I0780863

THE
FRAGMENTED MAN

ECHO SABLE

Copyright © 2025 by Echo Sable

All rights reserved.

No part of this book may be used or reproduced by any means, graphic, electronic, or mechanical, including photocopying, recording, taping, or by any information storage retrieval system, without the written permission of the publisher except in the case of brief quotations embodied in critical articles and reviews.

Table of Contents

CHAPTER 1

Disconnected Limbs

As winter's icy tendrils snaked down upon the city, its chilling grip was felt everywhere. Streets, once vibrant with life, lay eerily quiet beneath the relentless northwest wind. Cars crept by like sluggish beetles, and as midnight settled over the urban landscape, not a soul dared to venture outside. Rudi Wright stood guard by his glass door, eyes glued to the deserted streets below. A sliver of cold air seeped through the narrow gap, sending an involuntary shiver through his frame.

Rudi's 24th-floor apartment, nestled in the sleek confines of a new skyscraper, offered a spacious balcony accessed through a glass door. This outdoor haven, meticulously designed for coziness, was off-limits tonight due to the biting chill. Rudi chose to stay indoors, watching the few cars below as they scuttled through the icy streets, looking like shivering beetles in the cold night.

Minutes ticked by as Rudi lingered in thought. Just as he turned to retreat to the warmth within, something caught his eye—a pair of hands.

The hands, human and unmistakably real, clung to the platform's edge. Rudi could discern only ten fingers and a hint of the hand's back, as if someone dangled precariously outside his 24th-floor vantage point.

His mind reeled, and he blinked in disbelief. Surely, this was a trick of the light, an illusion. Who could possibly cling to the edge of a 24-story building in such punishing cold?

A chilling thought pierced his mind: a thief, but one either bold or foolhardy beyond measure. Of all floors, why scale to the 24th? If their grip failed, the fall would be catastrophic.

Rudi Wright blinked rapidly, trying to clear his vision. There it was again—a pair of hands, inching steadily to the left. Driven by urgency, he gripped the door handle and thrust it open, the wind slashing at his face with icy fingers, forcing tears from his eyes and momentarily blinding him.

In the fleeting seconds of blurred vision, Rudi surged forward, his voice poised to calm the unseen figure clinging to the platform's edge. He imagined himself shouting reassurances, urging the person to stay calm lest panic lead to a fatal plunge.

But as the words formed on his lips, they died in his throat.

He halted just short of the ledge, his heart thundering in his chest. The hands—those unmistakable hands—had vanished.

He peered over the edge, expecting to see a figure plummeting into the abyss below, yet the night remained undisturbed by any scream or sound of impact.

Rudi stood frozen, mind grappling with the impossible. His senses insisted he hadn't imagined those hands, yet now, they were gone, leaving only the merciless wind as a witness. He scanned the area, desperate for any sign, but found nothing.

Shaken, he hurried back inside, slamming the door shut against the chill of the night. With trembling hands, he drew the curtains, cutting off the view of the platform. He sat at his desk, but the sketches before him lost their significance, his mind preoccupied with the eerie image of those hands.

Three times he ventured back to the window, parting the curtains to gaze at the platform, yet each time the scene remained unchanged—empty, devoid of any trace of the mysterious visitor.

An hour passed before he finally sought refuge in bed, but sleep eluded him. His mind wrestled with disbelief, convincing himself it was mere illusion, a trick of weary eyes. Yet, as he lay cocooned in his blankets, a rare fear crept over him, the kind that made the solitude of night feel oppressive and the shadows more threatening than comforting.

The following night, an even fiercer cold gripped the city as the northwest wind howled with renewed vigor. As midnight neared, an inexplicable tension seized Rudi Wright. He paused his work, acutely aware of a soft "pat" sound echoing behind him.

Swiftly turning, a chill swept over him, as if he had stumbled into a frozen tomb. Nothing was visible. Suddenly, another terrifying "clap" echoed from outside the window, resembling fingers tapping on the glass.

But consider this—he lives on the 24th floor, with his room's window at least 240 feet above the ground!

Anyone creating such a noise at this height is impossible. It must be a hard-shelled beetle colliding with his window.

Logic insisted it was a beetle, but dread whispered of something far more sinister.

Rudi stood, shivering as the temperature seemed to plummet. His heart raced as he yanked the curtains aside, revealing nothing but the impenetrable darkness beyond.

Relief washed over him, the rational engineer in him dismissing the sound as mere coincidence. He returned to his desk, seeking solace in routine.

But the "pat" returned, insistent and unnerving.

Frustrated, Rudi glanced over his shoulder, the open curtains offering an unbroken view of the night. His blood ran cold as he spotted it—a hand, tapping rhythmically against the glass, its fingers dexterous and disturbingly real.

Paralyzed by fear, Rudi could only watch, his voice stolen by the sheer terror of the moment. The hand, a disembodied specter, vanished in an instant, leaving no trace of its presence. How it disappeared—whether by slipping away or retreating into the shadows—was a mystery he could not fathom.

His mind whirled, grappling to find any logical explanation for the hand's existence. It had appeared just below the final pane of glass, the owner hidden from sight, leaving Rudi with only an onslaught of questions and a growing sense of dread.

Who in their right mind would scale a 240-foot building in the dead of winter, tapping on windows as if in jest? The question gnawed at Rudi Wright, who found his thoughts straying to the supernatural. Though a man of science and reason, the inexplicable circumstances made ghosts seem as plausible as any other explanation.

Desperate to quell his unease, Rudi fled his apartment that night, lacking the courage to confront whatever lingered outside his window. He sought refuge in a hotel, where sleep eluded him, leaving him in a state of restless contemplation.

The next day, Rudi confided in Hugo Grey, a young colleague, sharing the eerie events of the past two nights. Hugo, amused and skeptical, offered to keep Rudi company, proposing to spend the night in his apartment.

That evening, the two men investigated the platform and windows with the thoroughness of detectives, probing for clues or signs of tampering. Yet, nothing yielded to their scrutiny, and Hugo dismissed Rudi's fears as baseless paranoia.

As midnight approached, the air sharpened with cold, cutting deeper as the hours ticked by. Hugo, initially reluctant to draw the curtains, conceded to the relentless draft seeping through the window. With the curtains closed, warmth returned to the room, easing their tension.

Hugo Grey, cradling a mug of coffee, prepared to declare Rudi's fears unfounded when the soft patter of footsteps echoed from the platform outside. The sound, though faint, cut through the stillness of the night like a knife.

The two men exchanged a glance, then turned their eyes toward the glass door leading to the platform. Hugo Grey, who had so recently mocked Rudi's anxiety, now found his own complexion ashen with fear. The long curtains blocked their view, obscuring whatever — or whoever—crept closer.

Hugo Grey and Rudi Wright sat frozen, their eyes locked on the pair of feet that had appeared beneath the shrunken curtain. The feet were clad in luxurious soft leather slippers and vibrant yellow wool socks—attire far too opulent for any common thief.

The question loomed: who stood just beyond the glass, separated from them by only a thin curtain?

Rudi Wright murmured, "No, no," his voice trembling as he clutched his forehead, pain etched across his features.

Galvanized by Rudi's distress, Hugo Grey felt a surge of protective resolve. He couldn't remain idle. Leaping from his seat, he yanked the curtain aside with a forceful tug.

But the scene beyond the glass door was empty of any human presence.

Hugo Grey's initial surprise turned to horror as he let out a piercing scream. The feet they had seen moments before were still there, but they belonged to no one. The disembodied feet, adorned in yellow wool socks and fine leather shoes, dashed away, crossing the stone railing and vanishing into the night.

Hugo Grey's scream seemed to go on interminably, his body shaking uncontrollably. He staggered back, grasping Rudi Wright's arm for support, his voice quaking, "Mr. Wright... Mr. Wright."

Rudi Wright, though shaken, managed to maintain a semblance of composure, his age and experience lending him a steadier nerve. After a long pause, he suggested, "Let's go to... your home for a night."

That evening, both men sought refuge at Hugo Grey's place. By the fourth night, their quest for answers led them to my doorstep.

Hugo Grey's father, an old acquaintance of mine, knew of my fascination with the bizarre and the inexplicable. Thus, Hugo and Rudi came to share their unnerving tale, spending an hour recounting the eerie events of the past nights.

They implored me to accompany them to Rudi Wright's apartment that very night.

Though intrigued by the mystery of these ghostly hands and feet, I was reluctant to accept their invitation. My recent marriage to Flora meant I valued time with her above chasing spectral phenomena. While the thought of investigating such a peculiar occurrence piqued my interest, I preferred the warmth and comfort of my new life with my wife.

As I considered how best to decline their unusual request, my mind raced to find the right words.

Flora sat beside me, exuding calm, while Rudi Wright and Hugo Grey faced us, their expressions tinged with anxiety.

I offered a reassuring smile. "I find your story fascinating, truly. But you must understand, ghosts aren't entities but rather manifestations of our feelings—"

I aimed to suggest they hadn't seen anything tangible, merely felt as though they had. Yet, before I could finish, Hugo Grey interjected, eager, " I'm certain we saw the feet. It wasn't a trick of the mind."

I spread my hands in a conciliatory gesture. "I'm not doubting you. It's possible that in expecting to see something, your minds conjured an illusion—a pair of feet, seemingly walking."

Rudi Wright, who had remained silent, now spoke with quiet conviction. "Mr. Morris, if that's the case, why didn't we see hands on the third night? I saw hands on the first two nights, so logically, Hugo Grey should have 'expected' the same, right?"

Their firm rebuttal left me momentarily speechless. I turned to Flora, silently conveying my apology for the inevitable night's separation.

To my surprise, Flora smiled warmly. "I'll come with you."

In that moment, I marveled at the simplicity of her solution. While I'd been crafting excuses, it hadn't occurred to me that we could face this mystery together.

Decision made, we soon found ourselves at the base of the towering building. Its grandeur was undeniable, but with only partial occupancy and its suburban isolation, it exuded an eerie emptiness.

We rode the elevator to the 24th floor, the highest residential level, where Rudi Wright's solitary unit awaited. The structure narrowed as it rose, culminating in his apartment, above which lay the rooftop, accessible only through a locked door from which the chill wind seeped, adding to the desolate feel.

Rudi Wright, a man who cherished solitude, had indeed chosen a serene abode. As he opened the door, I took a moment to ascend the stairs, inspecting the rooftop's iron-barred entrance. It seemed secure, an unlikely point of entry for any intruder.

Returning, I joined the others as Rudi Wright welcomed us into his elegantly decorated home. As a bachelor, he occupied the entire unit, complete with a bedroom, studio, and living room. Drawn by curiosity, I immediately approached the glass door leading to the expansive platform and stepped outside.

The platform was as Rudi had described—spacious and inviting, yet tonight it held an air of mystery. The cold wind bit at my skin, and I felt the weight of the night's promise hanging in the air, as if the very atmosphere anticipated the unraveling of an enigma.

I walked to the edge of the stone platform, peering over with a mix of curiosity and disbelief. The world below seemed impossibly distant, the pedestrians mere specks against the urban sprawl. The notion of someone scaling this height, grasping the edge with their bare hands, felt absurd.

Retreating inside, I closed the glass door, shutting out the chill. Flora proposed we play bridge to pass the time, a suggestion we all accepted. Yet, it was clear that Rudi Wright and Hugo Grey's thoughts were elsewhere, their focus fractured by the tension hanging in the air.

As midnight approached, Rudi Wright laid his cards down, his voice edged with unease. "Let's not play anymore, okay?"

I chuckled softly, trying to lighten the mood. "Mr. Wright, it seems like you're almost looking forward to it now."

But Rudi Wright's silence spoke volumes, his pallor betraying a deep-seated dread. Hugo Grey mirrored his unease, and even Flora's usual composure seemed to waver. An inexplicable tension gripped us all, stifling words and breath alike.

The quiet was oppressive, a suffocating presence in the room. Unable to bear it, I rose and moved toward the glass door, intent on dispelling the gloom. As I neared, I caught sight of what seemed to be three pairs of feet on the platform, startling me into near panic.

But then I laughed, realizing my mistake. The feet were merely reflections, cast by the bright indoor light against the glass. I turned to share the revelation, gesturing toward the platform. "Look—"

My words trailed off as I registered the expressions of my companions. Rudi Wright, Hugo Grey, and even Flora wore expressions of stark terror. Alarmed, I asked, "What's the matter?"

Before they could respond, Flora's voice, trembling with fear, broke the silence. "Oh my God, it's behind you!"

Heart pounding, I spun back to the glass door. What I saw was no trick of the light.

There, pressed against the glass, were two disembodied hands. They were men's hands, robust and masculine, with long fingers. A distinctive "cat's eye" ring adorned the right hand's ring finger. One hand was splayed flat against the glass, while the other gripped the door handle, futilely attempting to open the locked door.

I stood rooted to the spot, immobilized by shock. My mind raced, struggling to make sense of the surreal sight before me. What could this possibly be? I kept questioning reality, grappling with the incomprehensible vision that defied all logic.

Undoubtedly, it was a pair of hands, yet what exactly were they? My mind spiraled into confusion, overwhelmed by astonishment. Then, as suddenly as they appeared, the hands vanished.

A minute passed in silence before Flora broke the tension. "Did you see it? Did you see it?" she asked, her voice a mixture of disbelief and urgency.

Her words grounded me, and I began to regain my composure. Determined to confront the mystery, I asked Rudi Wright for the key to the glass door. With a click, I unlocked the door and stepped onto the platform.

As I moved outside, two theories took shape in my mind. First, perhaps the hands were a clever illusion, crafted from rubber and manipulated by steel wires — a feat possible for a skilled operator. Second, maybe someone dressed entirely in black was behind the glass, their body obscured by darkness, leaving only the hands visible.

But reality quickly dispelled both notions. The platform bore no sign of brackets or mechanisms that would support wire manipulation, save for a solitary radio antenna. And the idea of a person dressed in darkness seemed unlikely. How could they have retreated from the 24th floor so swiftly, without a trace? Even for someone with considerable skill, such a feat seemed impossible.

Dismissing these theories left me with an unsettling conclusion: the hands existed independently, belonging to no visible body. Could they be remnants of some otherworldly being, an entity whose form we couldn't comprehend?

Rudi Wright and Hugo Grey had witnessed feet before, just as surreal as the hands. I no longer doubted their accounts. But what could this mean? Were we dealing with some interstellar entity, whose anatomy mirrored the disembodied limbs of Earthlings?

Even if this outlandish hypothesis held merit, why would such beings wear rings and shoes — adornments distinctly human in nature? My thoughts swirled without resolution, leaving me standing on the platform for what felt like an eternity before returning inside.

Rudi Wright greeted me with a weary smile. "Mr. Morris, what is that?"

I shook my head, honesty in my uncertainty. "I can't tell you for now."

Hugo Grey, his face ashen, whispered, "Is it... a ghost?"

Again, I shook my head. "I don't think ghosts manifest as hands and feet. I can't say what it is."

Rudi Wright sighed deeply. "That hand tried to open the door. What did it want?"

A thought struck me. "Mr. Wright, do you recognize the hands? The cat's eye ring—does it ring a bell?"

Rudi Wright paused, then admitted, "No, I can't place it. I saw the ring, but if I'd seen it before, I'd remember."

I paced relentlessly, my mind grappling with the sheer absurdity of it all. This was no grotesque monster from the depths of space; it was something far stranger. Before us lay a pair of hands — ordinary, yet inexplicably unattached. They hovered, as if liberated from any earthly possession, accompanied by a similarly unclaimed pair of feet.

Time crawled by, each tick of the clock echoing in the heavy silence that enveloped us. Four figures, frozen, as if speaking might shatter the fragile reality we were witnessing.

By the time the clock struck three in the morning, the scene remained unchanged. Rising to break the stillness, I turned to Rudi Wright. "Mr. Wright, I'm leaving."

His voice was laced with unease. "What happened here—"

"I'll do everything I can to help," I assured him. "But for now, you shouldn't stay here. Let me take all the keys to this floor for safekeeping."

Rudi Wright nodded quickly. "Yes, yes, of course."

As he gathered his belongings, I paced a few more steps, the weight of the mystery heavy on my shoulders. Together, we descended in the elevator, leaving the enigma behind as Rudi Wright sought refuge at Hugo Grey's home.

Flora and I returned to our own abode, sleep evading us as we mulled over the inexplicable events. Our discussions yielded nothing but more questions.

The following day, I enlisted the help of spiritual experts, hoping they might unearth answers. But the house remained silent, its secrets locked away. On the third night, armed with a camera, we prepared to capture any abnormality. Yet, the phenomena eluded us once more—the spectral hands and feet never reappeared.

Weeks slipped by without resolution. Reluctantly, I concluded our vigil. I told Rudi Wright he could move back, but he chose to abandon that floor. Despite buying it in installments and continuing to make monthly payments, he left the space empty.

Then came Christmas—a time when the world seemed to pause, cloaked in a universal warmth. Flora and I accepted an invitation to a gathering that promised good company and a brief escape from our perplexing ordeal.

The chill in the air was biting that evening as we arrived at the party, hosted by a distinguished professor. Amid the mingling guests, the social pleasantries blurred into insignificance. But then, Professor Young introduced me to "Mr. Dunn."

Standing before me was a man, tall and imposing. He extended his hand, and as we shook, a jolt coursed through me, as though I had touched a live wire.

His hand was robust, adorned with a striking cat's eye ring — a gem of exceptional quality, its unique style unmistakably familiar. I had seen this ring before, its significance now an electrifying revelation.

On the platform where Rudi Wright once resided, I had seen that ring before. At the time, it adorned a thick, imposing hand—much like the one I was clasping now—yet back then, it was just a hand, unattached to any body.

My shock at recognizing the ring must have been evident, as I found myself holding the man's hand longer than politeness dictated. He withdrew it with a slight pull, prompting me to offer a sheepish smile. "Forgive me," I mumbled. "I suffer from extreme neurasthenia, and often find myself in a trance."

He uttered a noncommittal "hum" and turned away, leaving me to retreat into a shadowy corner, watching him from a distance. The man engaged in conversation with another guest, his tall frame and naturally curly hair lending him an air of elegance. He couldn't have been more than thirty, but his appearance revealed little about his character.

I observed him closely, unnoticed, until I seized an opportunity to catch the host alone in his study. Pointing discreetly toward the mysterious figure, I asked, "Who is that?"

The host seemed surprised. "Haven't I introduced you? Didn't you speak with him?"

I shook my head. "No."

"Ah," the host replied. "I thought you would. He's quite similar to you—a bit of a weirdo. His passion is traveling, especially to ancient Eastern lands, delving into their mysteries. He comes from wealth, so he can afford his adventures."

"And his name?" I pressed.

"We call him 'Doctor,'" the host said.

"Doctor?" I echoed, intrigued. "Doctor of what, exactly?"

"He holds numerous doctoral titles," the host explained, "from obscure universities in India, Egypt, and Iran. Theology, spiritualism, archaeology—you name it."

I took a deep breath, absorbing the oddity of it all.

What interested me even more was his hand and the gem ring on it!

Sensing my silence, the host excused himself. "His real name is Jax Dunn. Quite the eccentric. Apologies, but I must attend to the other guests."

I nodded, understanding the host's constraints. Alone, I sank into the sofa, my mind a whirl of questions about Jax Dunn. What was his true nature?

Resolved to discuss this with Flora, I rose, only to be interrupted by the sharp click of a turning door handle. The door swung open, revealing Jax Dunn himself.

Arrogance etched into his features, he regarded me with distaste. "It's unethical to discuss people behind their backs," he declared coldly.

Startled by his presence, I struggled to compose myself. His sudden intrusion and accusatory tone only added to the enigma surrounding him.

CHAPTER 2

Confronting the Enigmatic Stranger

His sudden appearance startled me, but it was his words that truly shocked. How did Jax Dunn know I'd been asking about him? Had the host betrayed my inquiries? The thought seemed improbable; the host wouldn't have mentioned it. So, how did Jax Dunn know?

I took a moment to collect myself, considering that perhaps he meant something else entirely. With a calm smile, I nodded, responding vaguely, "That's right, Mr. Dunn."

To my surprise, Jax Dunn's demeanor remained abrasive. "And you," he declared, "are quite the immoral person."

Anger flared within me. "Sir, I don't understand what you mean."

Jax Dunn's voice was sharp, cutting through the air. "I warn you—mind your own business."

I gave a derisive laugh. "I'll decide what I concern myself with."

His laughter, a chilling "hehe," sent shivers down my spine. The sound was unsettling, filled with an eerie malice. I stood, my face betraying the hostility I felt.

We locked eyes, a silent battle of wills. Then, with a contemptuous smile, Jax Dunn turned abruptly and left the study.

I remained rooted, struggling to regain my composure. The mystery of Jax Dunn had woven itself into my thoughts, an enigma that demanded to be unraveled. Who was he, truly? What secrets lay beneath his composed exterior, and why had I witnessed his hands in such an inexplicable manner?

The hands I had seen—disembodied, yet undeniably his—were not just a fleeting apparition. They were a puzzle piece, a fragment of a larger, more complex picture. The cat's eye ring that adorned one finger glinted with an otherworldly allure, a symbol perhaps, of something far greater than I could yet comprehend.

In the quiet of the night, as shadows played tricks on the mind, I pondered the possibilities. Could Jax Dunn be a master of illusion, a conjurer of realities that lay just beyond the veil of perception? Or was there a deeper, more profound connection — something that intertwined the realms of science, history, and perhaps even the spiritual?

My mind raced with questions. Could his time in India have gifted him with mastery over ancient magic?

Indian magic, renowned across the world, often relied on sleight of hand. But hands moving independently? That defied all logic.

Determined to uncover the truth, I resolved to study Jax Dunn further.

Exiting the study, I sought out Flora. Discreetly, I pointed Jax Dunn out to her. Her eyes widened at the sight of the cat's eye ring, and I quickly covered her mouth to stifle an impending scream.

"I plan to follow him after the party," I whispered. "You should head back."

Concern etched across her face, Flora protested, "I'm worried."

I chuckled, trying to ease her fears. "I've faced worse. What's there to fear?" Yet Flora remained uneasy. "I know you've been through a lot, but this person... this whole thing... it feels so mysterious. Maybe I should go with you?"

I shook my head, smiling. "I'm trailing someone. More people would only complicate things."

With a resigned sigh, Flora nodded, her silence conceding the point.

I offered Flora a few reassurances, though I felt they were unnecessary. To me, trailing someone with peculiar habits was a minor adventure, hardly worth the concern.

After lingering at the banquet for nearly an hour, I bid farewell to the host, citing an urgent matter that required my attention. He understood, not pressing me to stay. As I stepped out into the biting cold, the crisp air sharpened my senses.

I found a perfect vantage point behind a bush, from where I could observe anyone leaving the villa. Whether they turned left or right, I'd be poised to follow, ready to leap into action.

The cold gnawed at me, forcing me to jog in place to keep warm. After forty minutes of waiting, Jax Dunn finally emerged. To my surprise, he opted to walk, hands buried in his coat pockets, whistling a tune as he strolled casually through the iron gate, veering left.

His decision to walk made my task simpler. I let him advance ten paces before slipping from my hiding spot. As he neared a corner, I quickened my stride, ensuring I maintained a safe distance behind him. The festival's lively streets provided the perfect cover for my pursuit.

We weaved through the city, moving from street to street, until the landscape shifted to the quieter suburbs. Recognition dawned on me as I realized the road we traveled led to Rudi Wright's building.

The structure loomed ahead, singular and imposing. It became clear that Jax Dunn resided here. I slowed my pace, careful not to attract attention, and watched as he entered the building. Once he disappeared inside, I sprinted forward.

In the lobby, I caught sight of an elevator ascending to the 23rd floor before it halted. Moments later, it began its descent.

Jax Dunn's residence was on the 23rd floor! This revelation confirmed a connection to the mysterious events at Rudi Wright's home.

Armed with this knowledge, I felt a sense of ease. I stepped into another elevator, riding it to the 23rd floor. As I emerged, I was greeted by two closed doors, each one guarding a residential unit.

Determining which door belonged to Jax Dunn was the next challenge. More pressing, though, was the question of what to do with this information. Confronting him seemed premature, especially given his antagonistic demeanor at Professor Young's event. Gathering more evidence was the prudent choice.

Resolved to uncover the truth, I decided to proceed with caution, ensuring my next steps would bring clarity to the enigmatic puzzle that was Jax Dunn.

Having devised my plan, I ascended one floor and unlocked the door with my key. Inside, I quickly called Flora at Professor Young's house, urging her to come home swiftly and bring essential equipment. I assured her that tonight, we would uncover the answers to the peculiar occurrences.

Flora arrived more swiftly than anticipated, appearing just fifteen minutes later with the items I'd requested, including a microwave amplification eavesdropping device and a cleverly constructed periscope based on the principle of refraction.

Before her arrival, I had already pinpointed Jax Dunn's unit below the platform, the only one illuminated amidst the darkness. Once Flora joined me, we moved to the platform. I carefully extended the eavesdropping device's tube, allowing the microwave oscillator to dangle, and fitted the earphones into my ears.

I then aimed the periscope's lens at the window beneath us, but the thick curtains obscured any view. The suction cup of the eavesdropping device adhered to the glass, ready to transmit any sound from within.

Flora waited patiently as I set everything up. "What do you hear?" she inquired.

I shook my head. "Nothing yet. But I'm sure if we wait a bit longer, we'll—"

I cut myself off abruptly as a sound emerged, resonating like the steady beat of a muted drum. The rhythm continued for several minutes before Jax Dunn's voice cut through the silence. He was indeed in the room, which both confirmed our suspicions and piqued my curiosity further. His words were indistinct, as if he was conversing with himself. Then the rhythmic "da da" sound resumed, persisting long after his voice faded.

We listened intently, but the half-hour vigil yielded no further revelations. Impatience crept in.

"We're certain about the cat's eye ring," Flora remarked. "Since we know he lives below, why not confront him directly?"

I shook my head. "Not a good idea. He's hostile. It would likely lead nowhere."

"So, we just keep listening?" Flora asked, a hint of frustration in her voice.

Standing up, I stretched to ease the strain of prolonged crouching. "Let's take a break and rest inside for a bit. We can return later and might catch something new."

Flora nodded, and we moved toward the house. But as we took our first steps, we froze, eyes wide.

The glass door was opening. The wind whipped across the platform, but it seemed impossible for such a gust to force open the heavy door.

No, this wasn't the work of the wind. Before us, a pair of hands—disembodied and eerily familiar—pushed the door ajar. An uncanny chill gripped us as we watched the hands that belonged to no visible body, a ghostly reminder of the bizarre enigma we were entwined in.

The right hand grasped the door handle with a firm, deliberate motion, pushing the heavy glass door open. On its finger gleamed the unmistakable cat's eye ring. Meanwhile, the left hand clutched a porcelain ashtray, an everyday item from Rudi Wright's abode.

The hands moved with a coordination that suggested they belonged to a single body, yet they hovered in eerie autonomy. Flora and I stood frozen, pressed together in shock, unable to utter a word or make a move.

We watched in stunned silence as the hands completed their task, slipping swiftly past the stone edge of the platform and vanishing from sight.

After what felt like an eternity, Flora murmured, "It must be an incomplete invisible man!"

The idea of an invisible man seemed plausible at first. We couldn't see anything but the hands. But if it were an invisible man, why were only the hands visible? And how could they vanish so swiftly over the edge?

An invisible man would still have a physical form, even if unseen. If he fell from the 24th floor, his body would suffer the consequences of gravity. Thus, the hands' disappearance in such a manner defied the logic of invisibility.

These weren't the hands of an invisible man; they were just hands, independent of any body. Yet, what were they? The question left my mind tangled in confusion, resisting any rational explanation.

We remained silent until Flora broke the stillness. "Why steal an ashtray? What secret could it hold that's worth taking?"

Her question spun a web of new uncertainties, further clouding my already chaotic thoughts. Driven by impulse, I decided, "Let's stop guessing and confront him."

Flora hesitated, "Who are we going to see?"

"The 23rd floor," I replied, determination edging my voice. "We need to confront Jax Dunn—the one whose hands just took the ashtray from Rudi Wright's room!"

Flora interjected, "If he is truly invisible—"

I cut her off, almost brusquely, "He's not invisible, he... he..."

I faltered. What was he, if not invisible? The words eluded me, leaving an unsettling gap in my understanding. The truth lay just out of reach, but I was resolved to uncover it, no matter how elusive it seemed.

Flora, ever the supportive partner, took my harsh words in stride. She held my hand gently, her voice soothing as she suggested, "Let's take a break inside. Maybe a drink will help you relax."

Her understanding touched me, and with a tinge of guilt, I followed her through the glass door. We settled onto the sofa, and she poured me a glass of brandy. I sipped it slowly, feeling the warmth spread through me.

After ten minutes, my mind was clearer, but my resolve remained firm. I set down the glass decisively. "We need to confront him. Sitting here and speculating won't get us anywhere. Let's go."

Flora shrugged, a hint of a smile on her lips. "Do you think he'll welcome us?"

I replied with determination, "Whether he does or not, we're going to see him."

She stood, her confidence matching my own. "We've faced so much together. We're not afraid of him. Let's go." With that, she headed towards the door.

I moved to turn off the lights in Rudi Wright's house, preparing to leave. Just as we were about to step outside, a thought struck me—I'd forgotten to lock the glass door leading to the platform. I turned back to address it.

But as I turned, I froze, eyes widening in disbelief.

With the lights off inside, the dim glow from outside offered just enough illumination to catch sight of the platform. And there, a pair of feet appeared.

They jumped down from the stone edge, landing softly on the platform, and began to walk, step by step, towards us.

Flora noticed them too, clutching my arm in silent shock. Together, we watched as the feet approached the glass door.

It was a pair of feet, complete with calves, clad in soft leather shoes and woolen socks—exactly as Rudi Wright had described them. They reached the door, lifted a right foot, and pushed it gently against the glass.

The door swung open slowly, inviting the unknown into our midst. The sight filled me with a mix of dread and fascination, as the mystery deepened before our very eyes.

At that moment, Flora and I were utterly terrified, but I managed to hold onto a thread of logic. The right foot had pushed the glass door open, confirming my suspicion that Jax Dunn wasn't an invisible man. An invisible man would have used invisible hands, not a visible foot, to open the door.

The feet moved inside, the right foot leading, then the left, as they crossed the threshold. Flora and I were rooted in place, unable to do anything but watch as the feet stumbled around, bumping into the tea table and sofa before advancing towards us.

Suddenly, Flora screamed, and instinctively, I yelled and lashed out, kicking forward with all my might. My foot connected with the right shin of the disembodied feet, and I felt a sharp pain in my toes from the impact. The feet staggered back, visibly recoiling from the force of the blow.

The sight of the retreating feet, staggering as if in pain, sent a chill down my spine, like icy fingers crawling along my back. We were both dizzy with shock, unable to comprehend the sight before us.

When we finally regained our senses, the feet had vanished. I exhaled slowly, turning to see Flora's face, pale and drawn.

"Don't be afraid," I reassured her. "You see, those feet aren't so terrifying. You screamed, I kicked, and they left. There's nothing to fear."

Flora shook her head. "I'm not scared. We're whole people; of course, we're not afraid of a pair of incomplete feet. It's just... it's strange and nauseating!"

She was right; it was nauseating. But I couldn't admit it, not now. I had to keep Flora calm. Leaning closer, I whispered, "I know why you feel like vomiting!"

Flora blushed and turned away with a dismissive "pooh," easing the tension that had gripped us.

Pacing a few steps, I said, "I'll take you home first, then I'll come back to confront Jax Dunn."

"No," Flora insisted. "I'll go with you."

"No," I replied hurriedly. "Jax Dunn might be something we've never encountered before. It's better if you don't come."

Flora didn't argue further, but she didn't agree either. She simply walked to the door, opened it, and said, "Let's go down together."

With a helpless sigh, I followed her, and together we descended to the 23rd floor. Two doors awaited us, and based on the direction of Jax Dunn's window, I deduced that his apartment was the one on the left.

Standing before the door, I knocked, finding no doorbell. After a couple of minutes, Jax Dunn's gruff voice called out, "Who is it?"

Caught off guard, I hesitated, but Flora promptly answered, "It's an uninvited guest, but please open the door."

Jax Dunn's voice grew more impatient, "Go away! What uninvited guest?"

I pressed on, "Mr. Dunn, we met at Professor Young's dance party. I'm Ash Morris, and this is my wife, Flora. Please open the door."

Silence stretched on the other side, and I considered my options—force entry or return later with a spare key. But then, a "click" echoed as the door cracked open, revealing half of Jax Dunn's figure, his expression as arrogant as ever.

"I can't say I know you," he sneered. "What do you want?"

Flora chimed in, "Since we're here, won't you invite us in?"

Jax Dunn hesitated before stepping back, "Please."

He opened the door fully, allowing us entry, and we stepped inside, ready to confront the mysteries of Jax Dunn.

As Jax Dunn retreated two paces, the air in the room thickened, and both Flora and I felt our hearts race with an inexplicable urgency.

In that fleeting moment, the glint of a cat's eye ring caught our attention on his hand. He wore soft leather shoes, complemented by woolen socks, but it was the oddity of his gait that startled us—his right foot seemed to falter, almost as if it bore an invisible burden.

The memory flashed vividly before me: I had driven my foot hard into his shin. I felt certain that beneath the fabric of his trousers lay a bruise, a testament to our previous encounter.

Those hands, those feet—unmistakably Jax Dunn's— yet why did they appear to us, disjointed, like pieces of a haunted puzzle? What sinister game was being played?

We hesitated at the threshold, caught in the web of our own confusion, until Jax Dunn arched an eyebrow, extending his arm in a gesture that seemed more like a challenge than an invitation: "Please."

Crossing into his domain, Flora and I settled uneasily on the sofa opposite him. I had

braced myself for the bizarre, anticipating the macabre curiosities that might adorn his home. But instead, the room offered only trinkets of mystery—carvings from distant lands like India, Turkey, and Egypt, whispering tales of the enigmatic East. Artistic, yes, but hardly unexpected.

Yet it was the ashtray that seized our attention—a porcelain lotus leaf, innocuous yet undeniably out of place.

I recalled it vividly from Rudi Wright's residence, where it had vanished under the guidance of hands that seemed to belong to no one. Now it sat here, a silent witness to a story untold.

The room became a crucible of tension, words elusive, as Jax Dunn regarded us with thinly veiled impatience. The silence stretched, a taut wire between us, until it snapped with his sharp inquiry: "Okay, what are you looking for me for?"

The game had begun, and in that moment, the pieces began to fall into place.

I coughed, clearing my throat, the tension palpable. Deciding on a direct approach, I spoke crisply, "Mr. Dunn, we need to tell you that in the past half hour, we were upstairs on the 24th floor, in Mr. Rudi Wright's residence."

I expected some flicker of shock, some telltale sign of unease, for surely, knowing we'd been so near, he must realize we had uncovered his secret. Yet, Jax Dunn remained unfazed, his expression as cold and unmoving as a statue. "So what?" he retorted, his voice devoid of emotion. His indifference stunned me into a brief silence, but I pressed on, "I think we should have a tacit understanding, right?"

At these words, Jax Dunn shot up from his seat, his demeanor shifting like a storm. "Get out, you two psychos, get out!" he barked, pointing sharply at the door.

I rose as well, taken aback yet resolute. "Mr. Dunn, why react like this? We saw everything."

"What did you see?" Jax Dunn roared, an edge of hysteria creeping into his voice.

"Your hands, your feet!" I countered, unwilling to back down.

"Madmen, you're two crazy people!" he shouted, suddenly bolting out of the house, making for the door opposite. He furiously jabbed at the doorbell. What was his game now? The door swung open, revealing a middle-aged man in a bathrobe.

My heart skipped a beat. I recognized him instantly—a senior detective from the police force, Inspector Hale. I knew him well, though unaware that he lived here. Seeing him now, I felt a flush of embarrassment.

Inspector Hale seemed equally surprised. "Ah, Ash Morris, it's you. Mr. Dunn, what's the matter?"

True to his seasoned nature, Inspector Hale's gaze flickered from Jax Dunn to me, assessing the situation. "Are you unhappy?"

Jax Dunn glared. "Inspector Hale, do you know this person?"

"Of course," Inspector replied hastily, "he's well-known—"

But Jax Dunn cut him off, dismissing any camaraderie. "I don't care who he is. He barged in here, Inspector. I have a gun license. If I shoot him, it's self-defense, right?"

His bravado was undeniable, but I refused to be intimidated. "Mr. Dunn, you know what you've done!"

Jax Dunn's lips curled into a smirk, his knowledge of the law evident. "Oh? And what have I done? Be careful with your accusations, or I'll sue for defamation."

I had anticipated an unpleasant confrontation, but the reality was far more awkward than I had imagined. My impulse was to confront him physically, but Flora intervened, pulling me back as Jax Dunn hurled insults and slammed the door.

Flora and I exchanged a weary smile with Inspector Hale, who gestured toward Jax Dunn's door. "He's a strange one, that guy."

A thought struck me. If Inspector Hale lived next door, might he have insights into Jax Dunn's peculiar activities? "Are you awake, Inspector? I have something to discuss, if you don't mind."

Despite his hesitation, he relented. "Alright, I'm awake anyway."

We followed him into his study, a space lined with books and shadows. "Inspector Hale," I began, "have you ever noticed anything peculiar, like hands or feet that seem to appear and disappear, belonging to Jax Dunn?"

Inspector Hale frowned, his mind working to grasp the bizarre nature of my question. His confusion was understandable; these were not ordinary mysteries, and even I, embroiled in it, struggled to articulate the surreal events unfolding around us.

CHAPTER 3

Clumsy Espionage

Inspector Hale listened as I recounted the bizarre events that took place upstairs, yet his skepticism was palpable. "Those weird novels you write have clearly gotten to you. Be careful, or you'll pass this nervousness onto your kids!" he admonished, shaking his head dismissively.

Frustration bubbled beneath my calm façade. He didn't believe a word I said. Recognizing the futility of further argument, I stood, masking my irritation with a smile. "Perhaps you're right. But if you ever come across anything similar, please, let me know."

Inspector Hale, ever the diplomat, nodded absently. "Sure, sure," he replied, ushering us politely to the door. Once outside, I motioned upwards, signaling to Flora.

Without a word, we ascended and re-entered Rudi Wright's apartment.

Back on the familiar sofa, I lit a cigarette, the smoke curling around me like a shroud. Flora sat across, silent and contemplative. Despite everything, I felt no closer to unraveling the mystery. The fog of uncertainty was thicker than ever.

In past cases, I had always found a glimmer—a clue to guide me out of the darkness. But this time, though everything pointed to Jax Dunn, I was at a loss. The answers hovered tantalizingly close, yet remained out of reach.

The thought of breaking into Jax Dunn's apartment lingered, but his earlier threat was a stark reminder of the risks. Confrontation would only serve to alert him, and I needed stealth, not bravado.

After a prolonged silence, Flora spoke, her voice cutting through the haze of my thoughts. "Are you thinking of a way to uncover his secret?"

I nodded, contemplating my options. "I thought about sneaking in while he's away, but it's risky and could turn out to be a dead end."

Flora leaned forward, her expression pensive. "I have an unrefined method," she said, her gaze lingering on the floor.

The realization hit me like a lightning bolt. "You mean drilling holes here to spy on him below?"

She nodded. "Exactly. It's crude but effective."

I paced the room, weighing the pros and cons. Her plan was unconventional, yet its simplicity held promise. Regret tinged my decision; I had already tipped my hand to Jax Dunn. He would be on guard. But the situation left me no choice.

With a plan forming in my mind, Flora and I left the building. I mapped out the steps in my head, determined to uncover the truth lurking beneath the façade of Jax Dunn's unperturbed exterior.

The following day, I enlisted the help of a friend to acquire the blueprints of the building from the construction company. This allowed me to confirm with certainty that the rooms directly below Rudi Wright's residence indeed belonged to Jax Dunn.

I also consulted with another friend, a mechanical engineer, who designed a set of silent drills specifically for my needs. These drills, crafted from specially cast alloy steel, could penetrate the steel-reinforced cement with ease, and came equipped with a dust collection device to ensure that no debris would fall into Jax Dunn's rooms below.

This setup significantly reduced the risk of alerting him to my activities. Observing through a small hole would be cumbersome, so I procured four small TV camera tubes, custom-made with lenses that were just a quarter of an inch wide.

Once the holes were drilled, all I had to do was insert the camera tubes and I could monitor the goings-on in the three bedrooms and living room below from four separate TV screens.

It took a week to put all these plans into action. By the time everything was ready, the New Year had arrived. I hired a private detective to track Jax Dunn's movements. The moment he left his apartment, I commenced drilling in Rudi Wright's residence.

Despite having the most advanced equipment at my disposal, drilling through several feet of steel-reinforced cement demanded meticulous precision. Any stray speck of cement dust could betray my presence, so I proceeded with utmost caution, ensuring every move was calculated. I only worked when I received the all-clear signal from the detective, each moment stretched into an eternity, with the stakes higher than ever.

After two days of painstaking effort, I drilled the first small hole into Jax Dunn's living room—the very room from which we had been unceremoniously ejected.

With this initial success, my anxiety waned slightly. As long as Jax Dunn was out, I could proceed. Upon his return, I watched his every move on the TV screen.

On the first day of surveillance, I observed Jax Dunn limping into the room. My kick had left a lasting mark, and even after nearly two weeks, he hadn't fully recovered. He settled into a sofa, opened a briefcase, and rifled through some documents. His actions seemed entirely ordinary. After a while, he turned on the radio, filling the room with jazz music—an unexpected revelation about his personal tastes.

He lingered in the living room for nearly an hour before retreating to another room. I was left in the dark about his activities there, as I had not yet drilled into that space.

Two days later, I succeeded in drilling a hole into his bedroom, unveiling a startling secret. Jax Dunn's bedroom was unlike any I had ever seen—a place where the ordinary and the bizarre collided, hinting at mysteries yet to be unraveled.

Jax Dunn's bedroom was a paradox—a space that defied its very definition by lacking a fundamental feature:

a bed. Yet, it was unmistakably a bedroom, not by furnishings, but by function. For when Jax Dunn entered, he reclined not on a mattress, but inside a peculiar box.

In the living room, Jax Dunn appeared mundane, his demeanor unremarkable. But stepping into the bedroom transformed him into someone — or something — extraordinary. No one else would use such an unconventional resting place.

In the center of the bedroom lay a box, Jax Dunn's peculiar sleeping quarters. It was about six feet square, allowing him to stretch out fully. As he lay down, his face turned upward, I held my breath, fearing he might notice the small hole in the ceiling.

But he didn't. Instead, a bizarre expression crossed his face, one that defied easy description. It was one of almost euphoric detachment—reminiscent of a drug-induced high.

The box was intricately designed with multiple metal compartments, elevating Jax Dunn several inches above its base. These compartments, if imagined as razor-sharp blades, would have rendered a grim fate. His body, laid upon them, would be segmented—his legs severed into four parts, his arms similarly divided. His head would be detached at the neck, ears cleaved away. Of course, this was mere conjecture to illustrate the bizarre construction of the box, for Jax Dunn lay unscathed, a testament to the enigmatic nature of his sanctuary.

Observing through my covert surveillance, I held my breath, fearing he might notice the minuscule hole in the ceiling above. But he was oblivious, lost in whatever ritual this strange repose entailed. His serene, almost drugged expression hinted at secrets I was yet to comprehend, deepening the mystery of this man who lived so unorthodoxly beneath us.

The black-and-white TV feed obscured some details, but the box's metallic sheen was undeniable. It gleamed with an unsettling brilliance, capturing both Flora and me in its strange allure.

When Jax Dunn reclined into the box, both of us were left speechless. Flora murmured, "My God, what is he doing?"

I could only shake my head, unable to provide an answer. This was a mystery that only Jax Dunn himself could unravel. I whispered back, "Just keep watching and stay silent."

As we continued our silent vigil, Jax Dunn's right middle finger found a button on the box's left side. With a deliberate press, the box transformed. A cover slowly slid into place, sealing him inside completely.

My view, limited by the angle of the TV camera tube, allowed me only glimpses of the room's center, leaving the peripheries — and the walls — hidden from sight. What followed was a suspenseful wait as the cover enveloped him entirely.

Was there an air supply within? If this was a method of suicide, it was either ingeniously foolproof or tragically flawed. My eyes traced the wires trailing across the box's cover, snaking toward the left. Their purpose and destination were as mysterious as everything else about this bizarre contraption.

For two hours, Flora and I watched, the tension growing with every passing minute. When the cover finally retracted, Jax Dunn emerged, appearing invigorated, as if he had merely taken a refreshing nap. He exited the bedroom and moved to another space, leaving us with our questions unresolved.

Over the next two days, we observed this ritual repeated—a two-hour sojourn inside the box each time.

Flora and I had exhausted every corner of our imagination, yet Jax Dunn's bizarre behavior remained as enigmatic as ever.

Each time he ensconced himself in that box, he would "sleep" for precisely two hours. Then, as if guided by some unseen force, he would vanish into another room for an additional three hours, only to rush out with a haste that defied explanation.

We were certain that once the small hole was drilled through, revealing the secrets of that room, the puzzle of his odd conduct would unravel before us. As noon approached on the third day, Jax Dunn had left, and I was alone, engrossed in my task.

Flora had gone out to run errands, leaving me the sole guardian of our clandestine operation. I estimated that within half an hour, the drill would pierce through the mystery.

But then, the doorbell shattered the silence.

Setting the drill aside, I rose, stretching my limbs, convinced it was Flora, likely having forgotten her key. My hand reached for the doorknob with unthinking familiarity.

But as the door swung open, I was caught off guard.

It wasn't Flora who stood there, but Jax Dunn, his visage shadowed by a sinister grin that chilled the air.

I instinctively stepped forward, blocking the entrance. ""What do you want? You forced me out, so I won't let you in either!"

I couldn't afford to let him in. His entry would render all our efforts futile. I braced myself to push him away if he dared to advance.

Yet, another twist awaited.

Jax Dunn stepped back, gesturing toward the staircase. "He's here."

Before his cryptic words could sink in, three policemen, led by a commanding officer, charged up the stairs. The officer's voice boomed, "Stand aside!"

In that moment, I faced an unparalleled humiliation.

Reluctantly, I stepped aside as the police surged into the room, unraveling the truth. Escape was futile, for even if I fled, Flora, unaware of the impending storm, would be left to the mercy of the authorities.

In the end, my special certificate from the international police would safeguard me, compelling local authorities to lend their assistance. However, everything I had meticulously orchestrated within Rudi Wright's residence had come to an abrupt and irreversible halt.

Jax Dunn, with his cold, calculating demeanor, wasted no time in calling the authorities. The threat hung in the air—he could easily accuse me of infringing on personal freedom, a charge that would put me in dire straits.

I stood motionless, the weight of the situation pressing down as the officers methodically collected the fruits of my recent labor. One approached, his voice a curt command, "Alright, we need to take you in."

There was little I could do in defense. I nodded, resigned. "Fine, but I must leave a note for my wife, so she knows what's happened when she returns."

The officer paused, eyeing me curiously. "Does your wife live here as well?"

Alarm bells rang in my mind. A careless "yes" could implicate Flora as an accomplice. I chose my words carefully, "No, she just visited briefly. She stepped out and will be back soon."

"Alright, you can leave a note," he allowed. "We'll have someone stationed here in the meantime."

I scribbled a hurried message, detailing the day's events, before following the officer out. Jax Dunn, silent and brooding, joined us in the car, his sinister smile a constant reminder of my precarious situation.

Throughout the ride to the station, I maintained a façade of composure. Upon arrival, I was ushered into a small, solitary room. Minutes ticked by, the silence amplifying my anxiety, until the door creaked open.

Colonel Jack entered, the very picture of authority. His promotion from major was evident, yet the sternness in his eyes remained unchanged. He nodded briefly, "You're in deep trouble this time."

My voice betrayed urgency, "Didn't you inform Jax Dunn of my identity?"

Jack's reply was grave. "We hinted strongly, yet he's unfazed. Even if you were the police chief, he'd proceed. He's hired two renowned lawyers and claims to have irrefutable evidence. This case isn't in your favor."

The gravity of the situation hit me with full force. I was caught in a web I hadn't anticipated, and the consequences were rapidly spiraling beyond control.

Jack rubbed his hands together, his curiosity piqued. "You're interested in Jax Dunn? If he's committed a crime—"

I cut him off, shaking my head. "No, he hasn't committed any crime. He just—" I trailed off, a bitter smile tugging at my lips, unable to articulate the enigma that was Jax Dunn.

Jack probed further, "Why stop there? Is it stranger than the 'invisible man' tale?"

"In a way, yes," I admitted. "But you wouldn't believe me even if I told you. It's pointless to waste words. Is there a way out of this mess for me?"

Jack nodded, a glint of understanding in his eyes. "There is."

Eagerly, I pressed, "What is it?"

His answer was stark and simple, "Escape."

Escape? The notion was both absurd and tantalizing. Flee, merely over this? Yet, as things stood, it seemed the only viable option.

I hesitated, considering the unthinkable. "I want to speak with Jax Dunn. Maybe I can convince him to drop the charges."

Jack shrugged, skeptical. "I doubt it'll work, but you can try. I'll bring him in." With that, he left, leaving me alone to wrestle with my thoughts. What on earth could I say to Jax Dunn?

I paced the small room, frustration gnawing at me. Never had I imagined things spiraling into such chaos.

The door swung open with a "bang," and there stood Jax Dunn, his posture exuding triumph, a smugness that set my nerves on edge.

I had rehearsed a conciliatory approach, ready to extend an olive branch, but his demeanor sparked a fire within me, and my strategy shifted instantly.

Our eyes locked, and I spoke with icy resolve, "If you insist on taking this to court, what do you stand to gain?"

Jax Dunn scoffed, "I see no downside. A meddler turned voyeur deserves legal consequences."

I swallowed my anger, "But don't forget, I know your secret!"

He laughed, a cold, mocking sound. "You know nothing, poor fool. You didn't see a thing!"

His arrogance fanned the flames of my anger. "At least I planted a solid kick on your leg. Can you deny that?"

His face darkened, the smug veneer cracking momentarily.

I realized then that persuasion was futile, but a small victory was mine—I had pricked his pride.

He glared, words dripping with disdain. "Tell whoever you like. Who will believe you?"

The truth of his words stung. If I claimed in court that I'd seen Jax Dunn's feet kicking on the 24th floor, they'd likely send me for a psychological evaluation instead of taking my word seriously.

The irony was bitter. But at least, for a moment, I'd gained the upper hand.

In that tense moment of silence, a thought flashed through my mind like a beacon in the fog: the ashtray.

It belonged to Rudi Wright, yet somehow had found its way into Jax Dunn's possession. Regardless of how he might try to justify its presence, the fact remained—it was taken without permission. A seemingly minor crime, given that it was just a porcelain ashtray, but a crime nonetheless.

I exhaled, a slow, deliberate breath, and spoke with newfound calm. "Mr. Dunn, what about the ashtray?"

Jax Dunn's eyes narrowed, his voice a growl. "What ashtray?"

I pressed on, my tone unyielding. "The ashtray you stole from Rudi Wright's apartment on the 24th floor. I saw it at your place, Mr. Dunn. Displaying stolen goods so brazenly is a direct affront to the law."

His face darkened, the veneer of confidence cracking.

I shrugged, feigning nonchalance. "I could invite Mr. Wright and the police over for a visit right now."

Jax Dunn inhaled sharply, conceding grudgingly, "Fine, you've dodged a bullet this time. But let me warn you—stay out of my affairs, or you'll regret it."

Relief washed over me, and a laugh escaped my lips, light and unburdened.

Jax Dunn's voice cut through the moment, sharp and stern. "Don't get too comfortable. If you meddle again, you'll find yourself in deep water."

The laughter faded, and I approached him, my demeanor shifting to one of earnest curiosity. "Honestly, what's this all about? Can you tell me?"

He was caught off guard, unprepared for the sudden inquiry. "I am—" he began, hesitation halting his words. His demeanor shifted, turning cold. "Do I need to explain myself to you? Absolutely not."

Those two words, "I am—," hung in the air, tantalizingly incomplete. They could lead anywhere, yet led nowhere.

With that, he turned on his heel and strode out. I followed, the weight of unanswered questions trailing behind. As I exited, Jack approached, his expression a mix of concern and skepticism. Seeing Jax Dunn's stormy expression, he presumed I had failed, offering me a bitter smile.

But to our mutual surprise, Jax Dunn spoke up, addressing Jack. "Officer, I've decided not to press charges against him. Is that acceptable?"

Jack's eyes widened, a hint of disbelief mingling with relief. "Yes, of course," he replied, nodding.

In that exchange, the tide had turned, leaving more mysteries in its wake, but granting me a temporary reprieve.

With a dignified tilt of his chin, Jax Dunn exited, leaving the room charged with unspoken words. Jack turned to me, a sly grin playing on his lips as he clapped a hand on my shoulder. "You've really got a knack for this."

I chuckled, a hint of irony in my voice, "Please, don't flatter me. If I truly had a knack, would I have ended up here, hauled into the precinct?"

Jack's laughter echoed, a knowing "Hehe," escaping his lips. "Don't rush off just yet. Let's have a chat. I want to hear the full story, every twist and turn."

I hesitated, shaking my head slightly. "It's not that I'm unwilling, but I promised to meet Flora."

Jack's eyes gleamed with a shrewd light. "No need to rush. Your wife is already here, and she's filled me in on the basics. To verify her account, I need to hear it from you too. For now, it's best if you two stay apart."

A surge of irritation flared within me. I retorted, a sharp edge to my words, "What, are you worried we'll concoct a story together?"

Jack was quick to placate, "No, no, of course not."

Yet, I knew Jack too well. Without my side of the tale, I wouldn't be leaving anytime soon. Reluctantly, I recounted the events, each word measured, wrapping it up in under three minutes.

Jack nodded, eyebrows raised in surprise. "Is such a miracle even possible?"

"Indeed," I confirmed, "at least four people have witnessed these phenomena repeatedly."

Jack leaned in, his voice tinged with incredulity. "Every man has a fool in his sleeve. Ash, you're usually so astute, yet this time you played the fool. Had you informed us sooner, we could have deployed the latest wireless TV camera technology. Stealthily installed in Jax Dunn's place, it would have captured everything within a half-mile radius!"

I couldn't help but laugh at the irony. "If entering his house were that easy, why bother with cameras at all?"

Jack looked puzzled. "What do you mean?"

I explained, "It's simple. Jax Dunn's home is undoubtedly rigged with advanced security. Breaking in would be a dangerous gamble."

Jack pondered this before asking, "So, are you ready to abandon this pursuit?"

I laughed heartily, clapping him on the back with genuine camaraderie. "Colonel, after all these years, you should know me better!"

Jack joined in my laughter, eyes alight with curiosity and challenge. "Then let's team up. This mystery has piqued my interest too!"

CHAPTER 4

The Fragmented Mummy

In the intricate dance of espionage, cooperation can be a lifeline.

At least with Jax Dunn, it meant no sudden police visits. If things did go south, I would be tipped off in time to make a swift exit.

I quickly agreed, "Alright, but let's keep this operation small. Fewer people, fewer complications."

Jack nodded, understanding the need for discretion. "Absolutely. If it's just you and me, and nothing comes of it, it won't even make it into the records. It's as if it never happened."

I nodded, feeling a semblance of trust. "You—"

Jack interrupted, his mind already racing ahead. "We'll sneak into Jax Dunn's house. With our experience, evading his security systems should be manageable. Once inside, we'll install wireless cameras to monitor his movements."

The plan was risky, but it was our best shot. "Alright," I agreed, "but first, let me see Flora."

Jack led me to another room. As soon as the door opened, Flora rushed into my arms, her worry palpable. "It's okay," I reassured her, "we'll start fresh."

Flora exhaled, "I've been so worried!"

I chuckled, trying to lighten the mood. "Now, even Colonel Jack is joining our little surveillance mission. He's got some high-tech equipment. We need to move quickly though—Jax Dunn might relocate."

Jack nodded, urgency in his voice. "Give me thirty minutes to get everything ready."

He left to make preparations, and we waited, anticipation tingling in the air. True to his word, half an hour later, we were on our way, Jack at the wheel. Twenty minutes later, we stood at the entrance of Jax Dunn's building.

To our astonishment, the inept private detective I had hired, despite his glaring incompetence, stumbled upon us with unexpected news. Oblivious to the fact that Jax Dunn had already tipped off the authorities about me, he unwittingly revealed a crucial detail: Jax Dunn had moved out!

Apparently, just fifteen minutes prior, a large truck had been loaded with belongings and driven away. The detective had managed to snap a picture of the scene.

Despite knowing Jax Dunn had moved, we ascended to the 23rd floor, curiosity driving us. The living room furniture remained untouched. I hurriedly checked the other rooms.

The "bedroom" was barren, stripped clean.

The second room was similarly empty, save for an intriguing feature on the wall—four grooves. The upper pair seemed designed to accommodate arms, the lower for calves.

It dawned on us that if Jax Dunn could sever his limbs at will, these grooves might serve to store them.

But could such a feat be possible? Could someone truly detach and command their limbs at will?

Jack and I exchanged a look, a shared bitter smile acknowledging the absurdity.

We scoured the apartment once more, leaving no corner unchecked, but our search yielded nothing more.

Despite our best efforts, our investigation in the house yielded nothing of value. We had no choice but to rely on the photos taken by the private detective. Yet, once developed, they only deepened our disappointment. The detective had captured nothing but a large truck, devoid of any incriminating evidence. The contents Jax Dunn had relocated remained a mystery. These photos, worthless on their own, offered a slim lead—we could trace the truck's origin to discover Jax Dunn's new location.

However, our hopes were dashed once more. The truck belonged to a moving company, which reportedly delivered the items to a modest house, only to unload them and depart. When we arrived at the address, we found nothing but emptiness. Attempts to contact the house's owner revealed he had relocated to France, and the property was unsold, left in the hands of a real estate company.

It was clear: Jax Dunn had used the house as a decoy, switching vehicles to further obscure his trail. With the lead severed, our pursuit hit a dead end.

We questioned the movers extensively about what Jax Dunn had transported. Their answers were vague: the house was packed with boxes of various sizes, and they simply moved those boxes. The contents remained unknown.

Seeking another avenue, we reached out to Professor Young, since my first encounter with Jax Dunn had been at his home. Unfortunately, Professor Young knew little about Jax Dunn's personal affairs and was unable to assist.

In the days that followed, frustration gnawed at me. I was convinced that had I been granted more time, I might have uncovered Jax Dunn's secret. But now, he had vanished, leaving behind only a lingering enigma. For someone driven by an insatiable curiosity, this was a bitter pill to swallow.

Weeks slipped by with no sign of Jax Dunn. Colonel Jack had abandoned the pursuit, while Flora was preoccupied with preparations for the new year, dismissing Jax Dunn from her thoughts. I alone remained consumed, chasing shadows without success.

As the year drew to a close, an unexpected twist arrived in the form of a telegram. Its contents hinted at a new lead, though I initially failed to connect it to Jax Dunn. The telegram was from Myles Henry, an old friend and fellow scholar teaching archaeology at Cairo University. His message was brief and cryptic: "Something incredible has happened. Hope you come quickly to solve it together. Myles Henry."

Little did I know that this intriguing summons would reignite the search for Jax Dunn and unravel a mystery beyond my wildest imaginings.

"Incredible things" have always been my siren call. When I showed Flora the telegram, her response was immediate, "Don't pay attention to him. With the New Year approaching, you plan to leave home?"

Her skepticism was palpable, but I couldn't shake the lure of the unknown. I quietly sent a reply to Myles Henry, explaining my inability to travel to Cairo. Yet, curiosity got the better of me, and I ended the message with a question: What is this incredible thing? Can you share more?

The next morning, Myles Henry's reply arrived, lengthy and urgent: "You must come. This incredible event touches on the entirety of human history, the mystery of Egyptian mummification, and bizarre illusions of human body fragmentation movement. Come quickly."

While the allure of human history and mummies didn't stir me, the phrase "bizarre illusions of human body fragmentation movement" caught my attention. I had witnessed such phenomena before, and I knew it was no illusion, but a tangible reality. Could this be linked to Jax Dunn's enigmatic abilities?

I wasn't certain that Jax Dunn was the one who had informed Myles Henry about these "disintegrations," but the parallels were undeniable. I crafted a thousand and one arguments for Flora, outlining why I needed to go, countered by her myriad reasons for why I shouldn't. Our debate was as intricate and drawn-out as a United Nations assembly.

Ultimately, it wasn't the impending New Year that deterred us from traveling together, but Flora's father, Boss Sallow's deteriorating health. This legendary figure was nearing his end. If I left, it would mean parting from Flora. Yet, it was Boss Sallow who ultimately persuaded her, saying, "Let him go. Life is fleeting, filled with mysterious wonders. If he has the chance to uncover one of them, why hold him back?" With his blessing, I boarded the plane.

Upon landing at Cairo Airport, Myles Henry was there to greet me. Our paths had crossed many years ago during an archaeological endeavor in Central Asia. My enthusiasm for daily discoveries of lost cities had waned, but Myles Henry's passion never faltered. Now a renowned scholar in Asian and African antiquities, he retained the same energetic demeanor—short, dark, with eyes sharp as a field mouse's.

Myles Henry grasped my hand with fervor. "This journey will be worth your while."

This wasn't my first visit to Cairo. My previous venture involved a duel with a swordsman named Yupdo in the Arabian Desert and the discovery of an artifact capable of rendering animal muscles transparent. At that time, Myles Henry was engrossed in research in Azerbaijan, and we hadn't crossed paths.

I teased, "If this escapade doesn't outdo my last for sheer strangeness, I might just stop considering you a friend altogether."

Myles Henry laughed heartily, "Whatever you encountered before, it pales in comparison to what awaits now. You'll keep me as a friend, I assure you."

As we drove into the city, Myles Henry welcomed me into his expansive residence, more akin to a small museum than a home, located within the university's professor dormitories. Despite living alone, his space was vast.

Upon arrival, he instructed his housekeeper to prepare a meal for the cellar, a peculiar request. As we descended, a pungent odor assaulted my senses, nearly overwhelming. Yet, Myles Henry inhaled deeply, eyes gleaming with a strange enthusiasm. "This air is invigorating. Only in such an atmosphere do I truly appreciate life's value."

The cellar, despite its bright lights, exuded an unsettling aura, akin to stepping into an ancient tomb. All around were nearly eighty mummies, accompanied by sarcophagi and an array of funerary objects, each exuding a musty scent of antiquity, the air thick with the passage of millennia.

I glanced at Myles Henry, a hint of irony in my voice. "Professor, surely you didn't summon me from afar just for a meal amidst mummies."

Myles Henry chuckled, shaking his head. "Certainly not. Look here, these sarcophagi—do you see them?"

He gestured towards a massive oak work table, upon which six sarcophagi rested. One, in particular, caught my eye—a small, square, stone box, barely a foot across. The others were long and narrow, with one being especially large, measuring four feet in length and two in width.

These sarcophagi bore the wear of ages, their surfaces etched with the erosion of time. The lids were adorned with reliefs, though now blurred and indistinct.

Curiosity piqued, I stepped closer. "What's the significance? They appear ancient but seem rather ordinary."

Myles Henry shook his head emphatically. "Appearances can be deceiving. They are anything but ordinary. Open them, starting with the smallest."

Perplexed, I followed his instruction, pressing my hands against the lid of the smallest sarcophagus. It was a compact stone box. As I lifted the lid and peered inside, shock coursed through me, and my grip faltered. The lid slipped from my hands, clattering against the table and shattering on the floor, but I paid it no mind, my attention riveted to the contents of the coffin.

Inside lay a human head!

The neck was severed cleanly, and though it was a mummy, the preservation was remarkable. The features were distinct, the skin taut and leathery, still bearing the faintest traces of stubble.

The visage was striking — a broad forehead, a prominent nose. In life, this man must have commanded attention.

The head fit snugly within a groove carved from a solid block of stone, the sarcophagus crafted to cradle it with precision.

I stared, incredulous. "This is extraordinary. I've never encountered such a fragmented mummy before."

Myles Henry shook his head and stepped closer, retrieving the lid I had inadvertently dropped. He placed it back on the table with care before speaking, "You are wrong. It's not fragmented. It's a complete one."

I nearly questioned Myles Henry's sanity, but my curiosity tempered my skepticism. "Complete? But I only saw a head."

With swift, deliberate movements, Myles Henry pushed aside the lids of the remaining sarcophagi—"bang, bang, bang, bang"—revealing their contents. Only then did the full picture emerge.

This mummy was indeed complete.

In the two narrow sarcophagi lay a pair of arms, in the larger ones, two legs, and in the largest sarcophagus, the torso. Head, arms, legs, and torso — all present, yet disjoined, existing separately.

The sight of this fragmented mummy stirred a visceral unease within me. It defied the natural order, and I couldn't shake the thought that such a fate was the result of ancient cruelty.

I stepped back, repulsed. "What transgression warranted such a brutal fate?"

Myles Henry shook his head, a knowing look in his eyes. "You're mistaken. A body preserved as a mummy typically belonged to someone of wealth or status. It's unlikely this was a punishment for a crime."

I fixed Myles Henry with a questioning gaze. "Then, who was this person?"

Myles Henry explained, "I've verified that he was a pharaoh, albeit one with a brief reign. His pyramid is small, discovered by my team last year. We found no grave goods, only these five sarcophagi, arranged exactly as they are now."

The notion of unearthing relics from a bygone era intrigued me deeply. "What else did you uncover?"

Myles Henry continued, "Within the pyramid, we found a stone inscribed with the pharaoh's name, confirming his identity. His life is corroborated by historical records. He was a somber figure, solitary, with no known consorts. He ascended the throne at 26 and died at 28, leaving no significant legacy. Ordinarily, such a pharaoh would be of little interest, but—"

His pause piqued my curiosity further. There was more to this story, a mystery entwined with history and, perhaps, the enigmatic phenomena I had previously encountered. The prospect of unraveling this ancient enigma was both thrilling and daunting.

Myles Henry gestured toward the sarcophagi, his expression one of perplexity mixed with intrigue. "Why is his mummy like this? There's no historical record of a pharaoh being dismembered. According to records, this pharaoh died suddenly, and his uncle took the throne. Why, then, is his mummy divided into six parts? It's a mystery."

I mulled it over and ventured a hypothesis, "Perhaps his uncle coveted the throne and orchestrated his murder."

Myles Henry shook his head, dismissing my theory. "You clearly lack understanding of Egyptian history to suggest something so far-fetched."

His condescension struck a nerve, and I retorted, "Dr. Henry, I may not be an expert, but why, then, did you bring me here?"

Myles Henry chuckled, "Haha, maybe you've grown too accustomed to flattery."

Still simmering, I replied, "Flattery isn't something I often hear, but harsh words aren't frequent either."

Myles Henry, sensing my irritation, softened his tone and patted my shoulder. "Alright, let's focus on the facts. After discovering these six sarcophagi, I dedicated myself to understanding why the pharaoh's limbs were separated. I consulted leading surgical experts. Their findings were astonishing: the separation wasn't the result of any metal tool. The bones separated smoothly at the joints, as if by natural means. Remarkably, the blood vessels show signs of closure, intact."

I interrupted, disbelief coloring my voice, "What did you just say?"

Myles Henry reiterated, "The blood vessels at each incision appear sealed. The blood remained within the limbs, never spilling out."

I scoffed, "These experts must be mistaken. Such precision is challenging even with modern surgery, let alone thousands of years ago."

Myles Henry nodded in agreement. "True, they're aware of this, yet the evidence forced them to that conclusion."

I shook my head, grappling with the implausibility of it all.

"I've made countless hypotheses," Myles Henry continued, "but none suffice. I've kept this discovery under wraps to avoid accusations of fabricating the mummy for attention."

I pondered his words, "So, do you have any conclusions now?"

Myles Henry retrieved a diary from his jacket pocket and carefully presented a newspaper clipping. "Take a look at this news," he urged.

The article was laced with skepticism, typical of tabloid fare. It recounted a peculiar incident in Cairo where witnesses claimed to have seen two disembodied hands open a door and enter a house, though the rest of the body was nowhere to be seen. Crucially, the right hand bore a distinctive cat's eye ring.

As I absorbed the story, my mind raced, and Myles Henry's persistent questioning broke through my reverie. "What's wrong with you?" he asked.

I met his gaze, a realization dawning. "He's in Cairo."

"Who? Who is here?" Myles Henry pressed, his curiosity piqued.

"A person—" I began, but Myles Henry's impatience cut me off.

"A person, yes, but who? Why do you look so disturbed?"

Taking a deep breath, I steadied myself. "It's an incredible coincidence. Explaining it will take time. You should finish your thoughts first."

Myles Henry studied me, then proceeded. "This gossip made me entertain an extraordinary notion. Consider these separated bodies—could it be that he was dismembered while still alive?"

His hypothesis, bold and imaginative, didn't surprise me. Myles Henry feared ridicule, but I met his theory with calm agreement. "It's a plausible theory."

Encouraged, Myles Henry continued, "Historical records describe this pharaoh as intensely solitary. Perhaps he possessed some arcane method to detach his limbs— perhaps he was a magician. In ancient Chinese and Indian lore, there are tales of magic that could achieve such feats. This is undeniably worth investigating!"

I nodded, affirming his curiosity. "Myles Henry, your summoning me here was fortuitous. I, too, have encountered a hand unattached to any body, and a foot, which, remarkably, I've had the misfortune of kicking."

Myles Henry's eyes widened with astonishment. "You!"

"Yes," I confirmed. "Me."

Our shared experiences, though separated by time and geography, hinted at a deeper, more profound connection to the mysteries we both sought to unravel. This encounter in Cairo was not merely chance—it was a confluence of paths leading to answers long hidden in the shadows.

I recounted the entire saga to Myles Henry, sparing no detail. The story was inherently strange, needing no embellishment. As I spoke, Myles Henry's complexion grew increasingly pallid, and by the time I concluded, his face bore an expression of sheer disbelief.

For a while, we sat in silence, the weight of the revelation settling in. Finally, Myles Henry broke the silence. "This is incredible. This man, Jax Dunn, clearly possesses the ability to disassemble his own limbs!"

I nodded, adding, "And the mummy you discovered might have had the same ability."

Myles Henry tapped his forehead thoughtfully. "But I still don't understand. Even if someone can do this, what's the practical use? It's not like being invisible, which offers many advantages."

I shook my head, equally puzzled. "I don't understand either."

Myles Henry gestured toward the sarcophagi. "Perhaps we should put this peculiar mummy aside for now. There isn't much more we can learn from it. Our priority should be finding Jax Dunn."

I agreed wholeheartedly. "I've been searching for him for quite some time. Now, with new leads, I feel closer than ever—"

My words were abruptly cut off by a piercing scream from above. It was followed by the unmistakable crash of porcelain shattering, and then another scream. The urgency and terror in the cries suggested something had gone terribly wrong.

Myles Henry called out, "Housekeeper!"

Both of us dashed up the stairs, urgency propelling our steps. As we burst into the living room, we found the housekeeper standing there, face buried in her hands, screams still escaping her lips.

And then we saw the source of her terror—a pair of severed hands.

CHAPTER 5

Hands Stealing the

Sarcophagus

Before us floated a pair of disembodied hands, eerily suspended in mid-air, belonging to no one. Yet, I was certain these hands were Jax Dunn's. The distinctive cat's eye ring confirmed my suspicion.

The hands seemed oblivious to the housekeeper's terrified screams, continuing their slow, deliberate crawl along the wall. It was a surreal sight — hands moving independently, defying gravity. In the midst of chaos, my mind fixated on this impossibility (as the human mind often does, latching onto trivial details during moments of shock).

Myles Henry stood frozen, utterly bewildered. Clearly, this was his first encounter with such a bizarre phenomenon.

The hands paid us no mind, remaining unaware of our presence. They moved steadily through the air, inching closer with each passing second.

I was the first to regain my senses, having witnessed such oddities before. As clarity returned, I recalled childhood tales of powerful magicians. I'd heard stories of Indian street performers who would seemingly cut people into pieces, only to restore them whole. Legend had it that if someone caught a fly and removed one of its legs while the magician performed the trick, the spell would break, leaving the victim irreparably dismembered.

Of course, catching a fly was out of the question now, and the spectacle before us far surpassed any street magic. This was something else entirely.

What should I do?

Could I capture these hands?

The thought sent adrenaline surging through my veins. What if I could catch them?

As my heart raced with the thrill of the chase, I realized that capturing these hands could unlock secrets I had long sought. I stepped forward, and the hands seemed to sense my intent. Somehow, they knew, and they halted their movement.

I hesitated, startled by their awareness, and then lunged forward, reaching out to grasp one of the hands. The chill of its touch sent a shiver through me, colder than anything I had ever felt. But I held firm, determined to keep it in my grasp.

Suddenly, the other hand formed a fist and landed a swift punch on my chin, catching me completely off guard. The force of the blow sent me reeling backward, and my grip faltered.

Freed from my hold, the hands darted away with astonishing speed, escaping through the window. By the time I regained my balance and reached the window, they had vanished into the night.

I turned back to find the housekeeper silent and Myles Henry staring at me, his face ashen.

"They're gone," I said, my voice tinged with frustration.

Myles Henry's lips quivered before he spoke, "I... I admire your courage. That was incredibly brave."

I managed a wry smile, "It's not bravery, just clarity. I know these hands belong to a person, not some supernatural entity. It's just a pair of hands."

"But still," Myles Henry murmured, "such a pair of hands."

"We can't dwell on this here," I insisted. "There's a reason Jax Dunn's hands appeared. He might be nearby. We should search for him."

Myles Henry grabbed my arm, concern etched on his face. "These are dormitories. We can't just break in and search."

His words gave me pause. Even the university president couldn't conduct such a search without cause. I thought for a moment. "These hands will likely return. They must have a purpose, perhaps linked to the cellar."

As I voiced my thought, a loud "bang" echoed from below.

Myles Henry and I exchanged a glance of shock. The housekeeper, visibly shaken, attempted to flee, but Myles Henry stopped her. Another sound followed, a second "bang," less forceful than the first.

"Myles Henry, forget the housekeeper," I urged. "We need to check the cellar!"

Momentarily frozen by indecision, Myles Henry quickly followed my lead as I dashed toward the cellar. The door was ajar, and as we entered, the source of the noise became clear.

Two of the sarcophagi on the work table had their lids ajar—the one containing the body and the one with the head.

The body remained, but the head was missing.

The cellar was shrouded in an eerie stillness, its gloom deepened by the mystery of the missing mummy head. In this atmosphere of uncertainty, Myles Henry seemed lost, repeatedly muttering, "No, no!"

I turned to him, gripping his shoulders and shaking him firmly. "Yes, yes, the mummy's head is gone, taken by those hands."

Myles Henry met my eyes with a bitter smile as I continued, "I told you, Jax Dunn's hands had a purpose. Now it's clear—they came to steal the mummy's head."

Gradually, Myles Henry regained his composure. "But why would he need that head?"

I shook my head, equally mystified. "I don't know, but we speculated that Jax Dunn and this ancient pharaoh might share a connection, despite the vast chasm of time between them."

Myles Henry sighed heavily, "Yes, we entertained the idea that their limbs could be separated and moved independently. It seemed absurd."

"But we've both seen it," I replied firmly. "It's not just theory anymore."

Taking a seat on the sofa, Myles Henry held his head in his hands, grappling with the implications. Meanwhile, I focused on the fallen coffin lids. The larger one remained intact, but the smaller lid had fractured further.

As I examined the broken edge, I noticed a glint of metallic light from within the stone. Intrigued, I took a closer look and discovered a piece of black metal embedded between the stone layers.

The coffin lid had been meticulously crafted from two stones, concealing the metal within. Had the lid not broken, this secret would have remained hidden. Excitedly, I called out, "Myles Henry, come take a look!"

Myles Henry joined me, his eyes widening at the sight of the metal.

"What is that?" I asked.

"Let's find out," he replied.

We attempted to pry apart the stone layers but found them stubbornly resistant. Resorting to a hammer, we carefully shattered the lid, revealing the metal sheet more clearly. Despite our efforts, the metal clung tenaciously to the stone, held by an adhesive of remarkable strength.

The metal sheet, about a foot square, was thin and emitted a black, mica-like sheen. It was tough and produced a peculiar "clang" when tapped.

Once freed, we noticed an inscription etched into its underside—a strange script unfamiliar to either of us. The discovery shifted the mystery yet again, hinting at secrets and knowledge lost to the ages, perhaps entwined with the enigma of Jax Dunn and the ancient pharaoh.

After we fully extracted the metal sheet, the underside revealed a collection of strange characters. Myles Henry, engrossed in examining these symbols, seemed poised to unlock their secrets. Given his expertise in ancient Egyptian script, I assumed he would quickly identify them.

But I was mistaken.

After five minutes, Myles Henry lifted his head, confusion etched across his face. "Ash do you know what these characters are?"

His question caught me off guard, and I had no answer. These symbols were unlike anything I had encountered. They seemed more akin to patterns than any recognizable script.

I shook my head. "I was hoping you'd recognize them. If they were ancient Egyptian, you'd know."

Myles Henry confirmed, "Exactly. If they were Egyptian, I would identify them. But they aren't."

A new thought struck me. The presence of this metal sheet in the lid of the sarcophagus, where the mummy's head was once placed, hinted at a hidden secret. Had the lid not been accidentally broken, this metal might have remained undiscovered.

The missing mummy head could potentially be linked to this metal sheet. If Jax Dunn had indeed taken the head, perhaps he was aware of its existence and suspected it held a secret, yet was unaware of the metal's significance.

These were merely "assumptions," but they pointed to a crucial fact: Jax Dunn was central to this mystery.

I shared my hypothesis with Myles Henry. He paused to consider it before responding, "Your assumptions are logical. Our main task now is to find Jax Dunn, but—"

He trailed off, leaving the question hanging in the air. We both knew the challenge lay in locating him.

I suggested, "If my theory holds, Jax Dunn seeks some secret from the mummy. If he hasn't found it, he'll likely return."

Myles Henry, realizing the implication, asked, "His hands?"

I nodded and said, "Yes, we'll wait for his hands. Once they arrive, we'll carefully follow them. They'll eventually lead us back to Jax Dunn."

The housekeeper had left in fright, leaving a deeper silence in the house. Myles Henry and I sat vigilantly in recliners near the cellar door, anticipating the return of Jax Dunn's hands.

Although my hypothesis about their return was based on assumptions, we remained vigilant. I struggled to keep my eyes open, while Myles Henry succumbed to sleep around three in the morning. Fatigue clawed at me too, but I resisted, determined to stay awake.

At around four, my perseverance paid off. The hands returned.

It was a surreal sight—a pair of hands appearing as if from nowhere, deftly opening the door and gliding inside. I quickly stood, waking Myles Henry with a simple, "Here they are!"

Myles Henry understood immediately, scanning the area despite seeing nothing. I whispered, "They've already gone inside."

"Is it a pair of hands?" he asked quietly.

"Yes," I confirmed. "A pair of hands. They can't hear or see like us, but they react to their surroundings. We must be cautious in following them."

As I spoke, a series of "bang bang" noises echoed from the cellar. Myles Henry, anxious, suggested, "Shouldn't we get in to see what they're doing?"

I gently opened the door, "Let's observe from here. Once they leave, we'll track them to Jax Dunn."

Myles Henry's frustration was evident, watching his studio being ransacked from afar. Mummies were toppled, artifacts scattered, and finally, the hands focused on the sarcophagi. They explored each one, lingering over the empty coffin where the mummy's head once lay. Then, astonishingly, they lifted the sarcophagus.

The sight defied logic — a pair of hands, seemingly weightless, hoisting a heavy stone sarcophagus and floating it out. It was a spectacle that challenged belief.

As the hands approached the doorway, sarcophagus in tow, Myles Henry and I slipped into pursuit. Their burden slowed them, making it easier for us to follow.

We trailed them for fifteen minutes until we reached a deserted street. The early hour ensured solitude, save for a lone car parked nearby. The hands made a beeline for the vehicle.

My pulse quickened. Could Jax Dunn be inside?

Myles Henry and I exchanged a look, silently agreeing to quicken our pace, closing the gap between us and the enigmatic hands. The answers we sought might be just within reach.

The hands reached the vehicle first, tossing the sarcophagus through the open window before slipping inside themselves. We realized with growing alarm that thexse hands intended to drive the car away. If it escaped, there would be no way to catch it on foot.

Action was imperative.

I signaled to Myles Henry, and we bolted toward the car, but as we neared, the engine roared to life, and the vehicle began to move.

I had already formulated a plan: open the door and disrupt the hands' control. But as I reached for the handle, the car lurched forward.

Inside, I caught a glimpse of the hands gripping the steering wheel, accompanied by a pair of feet managing the pedals. A surreal sight—no body, just the hands and feet, yet sufficient to operate the vehicle.

The car accelerated rapidly, and I found myself running alongside, clutching the handle. Releasing my grip meant losing Jax Dunn's trail, perhaps forever.

Desperation fueled my resolve. I leaped, thrusting my hand through the rear window, hooking onto the interior and clinging tenaciously as the car sped on. Myles Henry watched, stunned, as I was swept from view when the car rounded a corner.

My mind raced. How could a pair of hands and feet navigate obstacles without eyes? The car's turning suggested some unseen force guiding it.

Twisting my head to peer inside, I strained against the wind and instability. But as I glimpsed the interior, a wave of terror surged through me, causing my grip to falter.

I tumbled free, rolling across the pavement until colliding with a wall halted my momentum. Dazed, I lifted my head in time to see the car vanishing into the distance.

The fear that had overwhelmed me wasn't due to any physical attack. It stemmed from the chilling realization of what I'd seen—or perhaps what I hadn't seen—inside the car.

When I looked into the car, I saw Jax Dunn's head.

Yes, beyond the disembodied hands and feet, there was a severed head resting on the driver's seat.

The shock of seeing a pair of hands unattached to a body was overwhelming enough, but it paled in comparison to the horror of encountering a disembodied head with a ghastly, corpse-like complexion. Yet, it was undeniably alive, for when I turned to look, the head turned to meet my gaze.

That chilling moment, the sight of that head looking directly at me, was what caused me to lose my grip and fall.

I've never considered myself easily frightened, but the sight of a living head with such an unnatural hue was beyond what I could bear.

After a moment, I managed to stand.

As I did, I heard the hurried approach of footsteps— surely Myles Henry returning.

He reached me quickly, concern etched on his face. "What happened? Did you catch it? I mean, why did you fall from the car?"

I shook my head, still reeling from the experience. I struggled to find the words to explain. "I saw Jax Dunn."

Myles Henry, sensing there was more to the story, paused before asking, "What did you see of him?"

I took his arm, urging, "Let's go back first."

We walked back in silence for a few steps before I spoke again. "I saw his hands, feet, and... his head."

Myles Henry nearly gasped, "His head?"

"Yes," I confirmed. "A head. Myles, I've witnessed many terrifying things, but nothing compares to a living head."

Myles Henry nodded repeatedly, understanding the gravity of what I'd seen. "I can imagine, I can imagine."

We returned to the campus and settled onto Myles Henry's sofa, both of us enveloped in a profound silence.

In such a situation, words seemed inadequate. The atmosphere was thick with fear and mystery, leaving us feeling suffocated under its weight. The bizarre events had thrust us into a reality where the boundaries of life and death were blurred, and it seemed we were only just beginning to unravel the terrifying truth of Jax Dunn's existence.

As the first light of dawn crept into the house, illuminating the corners and chasing away the shadows, we remained unmoving. The morning light brought a semblance of relief, a reminder of normalcy in a world that had become anything but. I finally broke the silence with a sigh, "I think we should give up on this matter."

Myles Henry shook his head resolutely. "No, you might choose to step back, but I can't. An ancient mummy divided into six parts, and now a living person who can separate himself in the same way — how can I not continue investigating?"

I hesitated, understanding his determination but feeling a growing sense of futility. "Of course, I want to continue the pursuit. But I believe we might never see Jax Dunn again."

Myles Henry's curiosity was piqued. "Why do you think that?"

"When I looked into the car and saw his head," I explained slowly, "it turned and looked back at me."

Myles Henry fell silent, digesting the implication of my words. He shivered slightly, the gravity of the situation settling in. After a long pause, he finally spoke, "Ash, if we assume he seeks a secret from my cellar and hasn't yet found it, do you think he might return?"

His question hung in the air, filled with both hope and fear. I pondered it, knowing full well that the peculiar events surrounding Jax Dunn were far from over. If his goal was indeed tied to some elusive secret, his return wasn't just possible—it was likely inevitable.

"Perhaps," I replied thoughtfully. "If he's still searching for something here, he might come back. But we need to be ready, and we need to find a way to confront him directly if he does."

Myles Henry nodded, determination flickering in his eyes. The path ahead was uncertain, but the mystery compelled us both to see it through to its end.

CHAPTER 6

The Mysterious Mummy

My mind raced as I considered Myles Henry's suggestion. "You think the secret Jax Dunn is after is the metal piece we stumbled upon?" I asked.

Myles Henry nodded, affirming his belief.

If Jax Dunn hadn't uncovered the secret yet, he might indeed return. But deep down, I was reluctant to continue. Claiming that we'd never see him again was an excuse to mask my dread. I wasn't a coward—many could attest to my courage—but the sight of that disembodied, living head haunted me. The thought of encountering it again made me uneasy.

Myles Henry pressed, "What do you think? Will he come back?"

I reluctantly admitted, "It's possible, but... I want to step away from this."

Myles Henry gave me a curious look. "That doesn't sound like you."

I shook my head, beginning to explain, "No, it's just because—"

I intended to say that his determination stemmed from not having seen Jax Dunn's head. But before I could finish, the phone rang.

Myles Henry answered, and his expression turned peculiar. He gestured for me to take the call. "It's for you!"

I was taken aback. "For me?" I repeated.

I'd been in Cairo for only a day, and it seemed unlikely anyone knew I was here. Who could be calling? I hurried over and took the receiver. "Hello?"

The voice on the other end was chillingly familiar. "Ash Morris?"

My hand trembled, nearly dropping the phone. I gathered myself before responding, "Yes, Mr. Dunn."

I emphasized "Mr. Dunn" deliberately, ensuring Myles Henry understood who was on the line. His face paled in response.

Jax Dunn chuckled. "Your voice sounds tense. We've met, and you've heard me speak, so there's no need to be frightened."

Words failed me, so I forced a dry laugh.

Jax Dunn continued, "I want to meet with you and Professor Myles Henry—"

I interjected, "You can come to us."

Jax Dunn replied, "No, I can't do that. I'll give you an address. Meet me there. We have much to discuss. You'll accept my invitation, won't you?"

I took a deep breath. "Alright, where is it?"

He provided an address. "I'll be waiting."

I recited the address to Myles Henry, who frowned. "That's a rough, secluded area. Why would he choose such a place?"

I wasn't concerned about Jax Dunn's choice of location. My focus was on deciding whether to go. The prospect of confronting him was daunting, yet the promise of answers to the enigma was compelling. The decision weighed heavily, and I had to determine the best course of action.

As I deliberated, Myles Henry urged, "What are you waiting for? Let's go!"

I hesitated, voicing my concern, "Aren't you worried it might be a trap?"

Myles Henry paused, considering my point, but his resolve remained firm. "Even if it is a trap, I need to know more. And you—"

I cut him off with a determined smile. "Don't underestimate me!"

Despite his unspoken reservations, Myles Henry and I left together, bound by our shared curiosity and determination to uncover the truth.

As Myles Henry drove, I sat beside him, the cityscape blurring past. Our destination was the address Jax Dunn provided. Once we reached the vicinity, we had to abandon the car due to the narrow, cluttered streets. Just as Myles Henry had mentioned, the area was indeed rundown and grimy.

Navigating through several alleys, we arrived at a decrepit stone house, the address Jax Dunn had given us.

While we examined the entrance, a young boy approached, speaking in halting English, "You, looking for Mr. Dunn?"

We nodded, and the boy motioned for us to follow, insisting, "Please, follow me."

Skeptical, I questioned, "But he asked us to come here to find him."

The boy merely repeated, "Please, follow me."

With little choice, we trailed behind him. He led us through a maze of alleys to another stone house, this one slightly more well-kept.

The boy knocked loudly, declaring, "Mr. Dunn, your guests are here!"

Our initial doubts about the boy's sudden appearance faded when we heard Jax Dunn's familiar voice from within, inviting us, "Come in, please come in."

Reassured, we stepped inside. The boy, having completed his task, was given some money by Jax Dunn and dismissed. The door closed behind us, leaving us in a small courtyard where Jax Dunn paced.

He greeted us with a nod, gesturing toward the interior, "Please, come in and sit down."

The atmosphere was tense, but the promise of answers pulled us forward. We followed Jax Dunn into the house, ready to confront the mysteries that had drawn us into this bizarre and unsettling world.

The room was tidy but modestly furnished. As a precaution, Myles Henry and I exchanged glances and waited for Jax Dunn to enter before following him in.

The centerpiece of the room was the mummy head, resting in the square sarcophagus on the table—a familiar sight, as it was the very item Jax Dunn had taken from Myles Henry's cellar twice.

Upon entering, I couldn't resist a jab. "What, did you invite us here to view the stolen goods?"

Jax Dunn sighed, his demeanor unexpectedly conciliatory. " Mr. Morris, can't we move past the hostility?"

His approach surprised me, but it also heightened my suspicion. I replied coldly, "Hostility? That began with you. Remember your warning at the police station?"

Jax Dunn dismissed it lightly. "That's in the past, isn't it?"

I was puzzled by Jax Dunn's intentions. His apparent desire for reconciliation seemed calculated, fueling my belief that he had ulterior motives.

Remaining cautious, I pressed, "We're here now. You wanted to see us. What's the real reason?"

Jax Dunn regarded me for a moment before speaking. "Mr. Morris, this really isn't about you. I need to discuss something with Dr. Henry."

His attempt to sideline me and drive a wedge between Myles Henry and me was transparent. Unfazed, I responded with a sneer, "Mr. Dunn, anything involving me is my concern."

We locked eyes for a moment before Jax Dunn relented, spreading his hands. "Okay, it's related to you too."

His feigned indifference only deepened my suspicion of his motives.

Finally, Myles Henry broke his silence. "What do you want?"

Jax Dunn paced briefly, gesturing to the mummy. "Dr. Henry, you've studied this mummy extensively. Surely you've uncovered its secrets?"

Myles Henry shook his head. "You're mistaken. I haven't made any significant breakthroughs."

Jax Dunn seemed genuinely surprised. "You've never investigated why the mummy is divided into six parts?"

"I have," Myles Henry admitted. "But I haven't solved the mystery. I hypothesized that this pharaoh had a unique ability to separate his limbs in life."

He paused, adding pointedly, "Like you."

Jax Dunn was momentarily startled but quickly composed himself, acknowledging the shared secret.

Myles Henry continued, "I believe you know whether my hypothesis is correct."

Jax Dunn offered a smile. "Dr. Henry, your hypothesis shows great imagination and intelligence. It's why you've achieved so much in your field."

Concerned that Myles Henry might be swayed, I interjected, "Enough flattery. What do you want?"

Jax Dunn began, "We need to start from the beginning. I know more about this mummy than Dr. Henry does."

Myles Henry, being a devoted "mummy fan," was instantly captivated. In his enthusiasm, he seemed unconcerned whether Jax Dunn was friend or foe and eagerly asked, "What do you know?"

I understood that interrupting Jax Dunn now might risk alienating Myles Henry, so I held my tongue and listened. Though not a mummy enthusiast myself, the mystery surrounding this mummy intrigued me.

Jax Dunn glanced at me, noting my silence, and continued, "This mummy belonged to a pharaoh with a peculiar nature. I believe he experienced something extraordinary that altered him profoundly—"

I interjected, "Wait, are you recounting facts or spinning a tale?"

Myles Henry, intent on hearing more, chastised me, "Quiet, let Mr. Dunn speak."

Jax Dunn sighed, "In that era, a bizarre phenomenon occurred. He became a being whose limbs could move independently. Such a thing was astonishing even by today's standards, let alone in ancient Egypt. To protect himself, he hid, but was eventually discovered. His limbs were found separated, leading people to believe he'd been murdered. However, when the pharaoh spoke, they deemed him a demon. Tragically, he was mummified alive."

The story was captivating, and both Myles Henry and I listened intently.

Jax Dunn paused, then continued, "Over two thousand years later, a similar fate befell another unfortunate soul."

I asked quietly, "Is that person you, Mr. Dunn?"

Jax Dunn nodded, confirming our suspicions.

Silence enveloped us again until Myles Henry broke it, "What exactly happened to you?"

Jax Dunn sidestepped the question. "I only know that someone shared my experience — an ancient Egyptian pharaoh. Though he is long dead, I must find him because I believe he holds secrets crucial to me. After extensive research, I discovered that his mummy was found and is now with Dr. Henry, so I came seeking what I need."

Myles Henry asked, "Is it this mummy head?"

Jax Dunn shook his head. "No, it could be a piece of paper, a stone, or—"

Myles Henry exclaimed, "A piece of metal?"

Jax Dunn's eyes brightened, and I realized we might be on the verge of something significant. The piece of metal we discovered could be the key to unlocking both Jax Dunn's mysterious condition and the ancient secrets tied to the pharaoh. The air was thick with anticipation, and I knew we were close to uncovering a truth that transcended time.

I quickly placed a hand on Myles Henry's shoulder, cautioning him, "Let's hear what Mr. Dunn has to say before revealing anything else."

Jax Dunn's gaze hardened as he stared at me, clearly displeased by my interference. He likely believed that without me, he could have swayed Myles Henry to his side. "So it is a piece of metal," he said, almost to himself. "And it's covered in writing, isn't it?"

Despite our lack of response, he seemed confident in his deduction.

He began pacing, emphasizing, "I am willing to pay any price for that piece of metal, any price."

His insistence was telling. It was clear the metal held immense value to him. Myles Henry and I exchanged a knowing look. We had leverage—the metal was our trump card.

As long as we held onto it, Jax Dunn couldn't act against us. While we didn't yet understand its significance, we knew Jax Dunn desired it desperately. I gestured to Myles Henry that I would handle the negotiations. "What do you mean by any price?" I asked.

Jax Dunn quickly replied, "Name your terms. I own seven tin mines and three rubber plantations in Malaysia, which I'm willing to trade."

His offer confirmed the metal's extreme importance. No one would exchange such valuable assets lightly.

Before I could respond, he added, "And a tea plantation in Ceylon."

I shook my head, "Mr. Dunn, you're speaking of wealth and possessions. Even if you offered a diamond mine in South Africa, we wouldn't be persuaded."

Myles Henry nodded in agreement, reinforcing my stance.

Jax Dunn's eyes widened in disbelief, "Then... what do you want?"

I stood and paced, considering my words carefully. "Mr. Dunn, let's be transparent. We want nothing less than all your secrets."

His complexion paled, and his eyes brimmed with an intense hatred, fixing on me with a chilling intensity that made my skin crawl.

I took a steadying breath and continued, "We want you to recount everything from your first unusual experience to now, leaving nothing out. Then, we—"

I halted mid-sentence.

The reason for my abrupt stop wasn't an interruption. It was the realization that continuing would be futile; the fury and animosity in Jax Dunn's eyes were palpable. Continuing would only escalate the situation.

A heavy silence settled in the room, each of us weighing the implications of what had been said and unsaid. The tension was thick, and it was clear that the next move could redefine our understanding of the extraordinary events surrounding us.

The tension in the room was palpable, and Myles Henry and I maintained our distance, wary of Jax Dunn's unpredictable demeanor. His expression was so unnerving that we half-expected his head to detach and attack us.

After a prolonged silence, Jax Dunn spoke slowly, "If you don't accept my terms now, you'll regret it."

I replied bluntly, "If you don't accept our terms now, you'll regret it. In fact, to prevent further disputes, we've decided to destroy the metal piece immediately."

Jax Dunn's reaction was immediate and visceral, "No!"

I met his outburst with a cold, "Yes."

His breath came in labored gasps as he tried to tempt us again, "You don't need to worry about my Southeast Asian assets. Properly managed, they can yield over $6 million annually."

I shook my head, unwavering. "Professor Henry and I aren't in need of money. Don't waste your breath."

Pressing his hands firmly on the table, Jax Dunn leaned forward, his gaze intense and menacing. "The secret I possess is beyond your understanding. It's too valuable to be dismissed."

He paused, then continued, "I can have the transfer documents prepared for my Southeast Asian holdings. My lawyer will handle everything."

Jax Dunn, in yet another flamboyant display, flaunted an exorbitant sum of money, trying to impress us. In unison, Henry and I rose, declaring, "In that case, we're leaving."

Our departure was deliberate, a calculated move to incite Jax Dunn's ire. And incite it did. However, what followed was far from what we anticipated. Instead of capitulating and revealing his closely guarded secrets, Jax Dunn's anger took an unforeseen turn.

"Don't go!" he bellowed.

As we spun around, we were met with a chilling sight. Jax Dunn stood, a German military pistol clutched in his hand, its lethal potential unmistakably apparent.

The room seemed to shrink around us, the threat now tangible.

I froze, realizing the gravity of the situation, while Myles Henry's voice rang out sternly, "What do you intend to do?"

The stakes had escalated, and the air was charged with a mix of fear and defiance. We had underestimated the lengths to which Jax Dunn would go to protect his secrets, and now we faced a perilous confrontation.

Jax Dunn's face was contorted with desperation and anger. "You refuse to help me, leaving me with no options. I'm at a dead end, and only you can save me, but you won't, so we'll all perish together."

I met his eyes, trying to understand. "You're at a dead end? What does that mean? You won't share your experience, yet you accuse us of not helping. How is that fair?"

Jax Dunn, fraught with tension, demanded, "Alright, I've laid it all out for you—I've hit a dead end. Now, hand over the metal piece!"

I placed a protective hand on Myles Henry's arm, pulling him behind me as I urged, "Explain why you're at a dead end."

But Jax Dunn's frustration boiled over. "I won't tell you. I won't!"

At that moment, I acted on instinct. I pushed Myles Henry back with my arm, sending him crashing through the door behind us. I followed suit, diving back just as gunshots rang out.

The sound was deafening, drowning out everything else as we scrambled to escape. We bolted down the street, adrenaline propelling us forward until we managed to jump onto a passing streetcar, instructing the driver to take us back to Myles Henry's dormitory.

Once we were safely inside, I urged, "Quick, grab the metal sheet. We need to hide."

Myles Henry hesitated. "But where? I have responsibilities at the university. I can't just leave everything—"

I cut him off, urgency in my voice. "No time to argue. Trust me on this."

With the metal sheet in hand, we hurried back into the city and checked into a hotel, where Myles Henry arranged to take leave from his duties.

My plan was simple: with Jax Dunn at a dead end, he would eventually seek us out again. But next time, his approach might be more conciliatory.

Over the next three days, we stayed put, reading about the "mysterious gunshot" incident in the newspaper. We speculated endlessly about Jax Dunn's bizarre predicament, but our theories led nowhere.

On the fourth morning, while I was in the shower, I thought I heard a knock at the door. Assuming it was housekeeping, I didn't give it much thought. Myles Henry was smart and capable; he'd handle it.

But when I emerged from the bathroom, a sense of dread washed over me.

Myles Henry was gone. The room was in disarray, his bed showing signs of a struggle. The door hung ajar, a silent testament to the chaos that had ensued.

Panic set in. Something had happened, and I needed to find Myles Henry before it was too late. The stakes were higher than ever, and I had to uncover the truth behind Jax Dunn's enigmatic and dangerous game.

"Myles! Myles Henry!" I called out, urgency lacing my voice.

I barely took the time to wrap myself in a bathrobe before heading for the door. Before I could step out, a knock echoed from the other side. "Come in, it's open," I called, breathless.

The waiter entered, familiar yet now a harbinger of unsettling news. "Where's Mr. Henry? Where did he go?" I demanded.

"We're not sure," the waiter replied, unease in his eyes. "He seemed... possessed, as if driven by unseen forces. He staggered to the elevator. I tried to follow, but he pushed me away. Is he... intoxicated?"

The weight of the situation pressed down on me. "Was he alone?" I asked, voice tight with concern.

"Yes, alone, but... it's hard to explain," the waiter hesitated.

I shrugged off my bathrobe, urgency propelling me, urging him, "Just tell me what you think."

With a reluctant sigh, the waiter confessed, "If the manager hears of this, I'll be in trouble. But Mr. Henry seemed compelled, as if invisible hands guided him into the elevator."

Jax Dunn. It had to be Jax Dunn! "Did you see anything—a pair of hands, a threat against Mr. Henry?" I pressed.

The waiter's gaze turned incredulous, as if I'd spoken of ghosts. Anyone sane would react the same way.

I fell silent, turning my attention to the oil painting on the wall—a seemingly innocuous piece. But behind its frame, hidden, lay a metal sheet we had concealed upon arrival. The painting's position was unchanged; the corners still aligned with our secret markings.

I dressed swiftly, urgency fueling my movements, and bolted from the room.

The waiter stepped back, and I, bypassing the elevator, flew down the stairs two at a time.

Outside the hotel, the weight of uncertainty settled upon me, a tangible dread tightening its grip.

Myles Henry had vanished into the sprawling labyrinth of Cairo, a city vast and teeming with life. Finding him seemed as futile as chasing shadows. Desperation propelled me across the road, scanning for any sign, any clue. My search was fruitless, the bustling streets swallowing any trace of him.

In a last-ditch effort, I approached a traffic policeman, hoping he might have noticed a short Asian man leaving the hotel in a peculiar state. His response was curt, dismissive— "No, no, can't you see I'm busy?"—a dead end.

Defeated, I retreated to the pavement. Just then, an elderly woman with a bamboo basket approached, her gaze fixed intently on me. She had the air of a street vendor, ordinary and unassuming.

I turned away, but her words caught me off guard: "Are you looking for a Asian man named Henry?"

Startled, I scrutinized her. She seemed genuine, not some actor in disguise. "Yes," I replied cautiously. "And you are...?"

She smiled cryptically. "I know where he is. But information comes at a price."

I slipped a large bill into her basket. Her eyes lit up with satisfaction. "A good man, your friend," she mused, "but a pity about his hands."

Her cryptic talk was grating, yet it piqued my curiosity. Her mention of "the man" could only mean Jax Dunn—a figure whose hands, though not physically broken, had metaphorically reached out to seize Myles Henry.

"Tell me where!" I urged, urgency sharpening my voice.

The old woman pointed down a lengthy, straight road. "Keep walking. You might just find him."

I pressed for more details, but she offered none. With no other leads, I dashed forward, heart pounding. Myles Henry, a scholar, was no match for someone like Jax Dunn. His life could be in peril.

As I sped along the road, I puzzled over the old woman's vague directions. Why would I meet him simply by going forward?

After about half a mile, a voice pierced through the air: "Mr. Morris! Mr. Morris!" The call was desperate and insistent.

I raced toward the source, finding a man who looked relieved to see me. "You're calling for me? Did someone send you?"

He nodded, visibly relieved. "Luckily you appeared! Or I'd have shouted myself hoarse!"

Here, at last, was a thread to follow through the maze.

CHAPTER 7

Caught a Dead Hand

The man slipped a folded paper into my hand, his actions as swift as his departure. I unfolded it to reveal an address, unfamiliar and cryptic. With no time to waste, I hailed a streetcar, thrusting the paper at the driver.

He frowned, a crease of doubt marring his forehead. "This is a very far place."

I pressed a generous banknote into his hand. "Take me there."

Money, that universal persuader, worked its magic. The driver nodded and we sped off, the cityscape blurring into a mosaic of colors and sounds. True to his word, the journey was long, nearly an hour before we halted in front of a small, pristine white house.

The house was an oasis of tranquility and elegance amidst Cairo's bustling chaos, a residence that whispered of wealth and secrecy. Its doors and windows were sealed tight, giving no hint of life within. But I'd come this far; turning back wasn't an option.

I stepped out, approached the entrance, and pressed the doorbell. Almost instantly, the door swung open to reveal an Egyptian servant, his demeanor respectful and inviting. He ushered me inside.

The interior was lavish, each piece of furniture a relic of antiquity, casting an eerie atmosphere. I settled onto a plush, expansive sofa, the servant disappearing into the shadows. The minutes dragged on, and impatience gnawed at me. Then, without warning, a voice crackled from the armrest—Jax Dunn's unmistakable timbre.

"Mr. Morris, you're here. Apologies for the wait."

The unexpected voice startled me, though I quickly recognized it as a mere transmitter, a trick unworthy of surprise. Jax Dunn's voice confirmed my suspicions. "So, it's you," I replied, my tone edged with anger.

"Indeed, Mr. Morris," Jax Dunn continued smoothly. "Your reluctance to cooperate has forced my hand. Dr. Henry is in a secure location, and only you can decide his fate."

His words hung heavy in the air, a chilling reminder of the stakes at play.

Damn Jax Dunn! The tables had turned. He once sought our terms, but now I was forced to bow to his demands, with Myles Henry held captive in his grasp.

I paused, weighing my options, then asked, "What are your terms?"

His response was as icy as it was expected: "The piece of metal."

Silence enveloped me, the situation precarious. Myles Henry was more than a friend; he was an old ally. I had to exhaust every avenue to rescue him from Jax Dunn's clutches.

I was certain that surrendering the metal would indeed secure Myles Henry's release. Yet, the dilemma loomed large — handing over the metal meant relinquishing any chance of uncovering Jax Dunn's secrets. Once freed, Myles Henry would realize his liberty was bought at the cost of that crucial metal, and might sever ties with me, the truth forever out of reach.

Finally, I ventured, "Is there another way?"

"None," Jax Dunn replied with finality. "That metal is useless to you. Surrender it, and your friend walks free."

I attempted to stall, "That metal isn't entirely worthless to me. It once held substantial value."

Jax Dunn chuckled, a sound devoid of warmth. "But you squandered that opportunity."

I rapped my forehead in frustration, an idea sparking. What if I deciphered the metal's secret before relinquishing it? I needed time. "Give me time to consider."

I meant days, yet Jax Dunn countered, "Very well. Ten minutes."

I shot to my feet, incredulous. "Ten minutes? Are you serious?"

His voice remained maddeningly calm. "You're known for your decisiveness. If you agree, do so now. If not, a year won't change your mind."

Anger flared. "Fine, if this fails, I'll involve the police and see how you handle it."

Jax Dunn's reply was disturbingly serene. "I have nothing to lose. Pity Dr. Henry for having a friend like you."

I inhaled deeply, steadying myself. "Jax Dunn, if you'd level with me—share the challenges you're facing—I might be able to help."

The air hung heavy with the weight of unspoken truths, a fragile bridge between ally and adversary.

Jax Dunn's threat was as chilling as the steel of his gun. "I don't need your pity. Ten minutes, or I won't hesitate to shoot you, then deal with Myles Henry. Killing one is no different from killing two."

He left no room for negotiation. "Start from now."

His eyes, wild with a mix of desperation and madness, told me he meant every word. I had ten minutes—a mere heartbeat of time.

I stood within striking distance of his pistol, the cold barrel a silent promise of death. He had me cornered with no visible escape, his extortion seemingly airtight.

Yet, surrender was not an option. I began to pace, hoping to buy time, but Jax Dunn halted me with a curt command. "You can stand and think."

My focus shifted to his gun, calculating how I might wrest it from him. But then, the unexpected unfolded.

A strangled noise emanated from Jax Dunn's throat, a precursor to the bizarre. His wrist emitted a creaking sound, reminiscent of a tightly screwed bottle cap being forced open.

To my astonishment, his right hand detached from his wrist, floating upward. The hand, still clutching the pistol, ascended until it hovered near the ceiling, the muzzle unwaveringly aimed at me. My eyes tracked its ascent, my neck stiffening with the unnatural angle.

Jax Dunn stood there, a man divided — his body separate from the hand yet still in control, the gun an extension of his will.

His voice, as detached as his hand, broke the surreal silence. "Nine minutes!"

The clock was ticking, each second an echo of the danger looming over me.

Only a minute had elapsed, yet it felt like an eternity.

I faced Jax Dunn, his expression a storm of malevolence. "Did you see that? Resistance is futile. If you don't comply in ten minutes, you die."

His words, dripping with disdain, carried a chilling truth. He had the upper hand—literally.

If his hand had remained attached, I might have chanced a daring maneuver to seize the gun. I've turned the tables in dire situations before, snatching weapons with precision and speed. But now, with his hand floating high, the gun pointed unwaveringly at me, any such attempt felt impossible.

Nausea churned within me as I muttered, "What... is this sorcery?"

Jax Dunn let out a peculiar laugh. "Don't you see? I am a fragmented person."

"Fragmented person?" I echoed, the term alien to my ears.

I took a deep breath, grounding myself. Jax Dunn's countdown continued relentlessly. "Seven minutes."

"How can you do this?" I challenged, incredulous. "Surely, you're the only one of your kind. It's... revolting."

His sneer was palpable. "Call it what you will. I am a fragmented person beyond your reckoning. Six minutes!"

I stepped back, and as I did, the floating hand adjusted its aim. Escape was impossible.

"Five minutes," Jax Dunn intoned, his voice a metronome of impending doom.

My mind raced, a kaleidoscope of plans and possibilities. Jax Dunn's reminders marked the passage of time until the final, ominous minute.

A sharp "click" echoed from above—the safety of the gun disengaged.

"Okay, you win," I conceded hastily.

His response was immediate. "Bring it here."

"It's not with me. I need to retrieve it," I replied, my voice steady.

"Fine. I'll accompany you," Jax Dunn agreed, as I suspected he would.

I had no intention of surrendering. This was a strategic retreat. With Jax Dunn accompanying me, opportunities might arise. I had to believe that.

I glanced up. His hand remained, a sinister sentinel. "Turn around and lower your head," Jax Dunn ordered.

I had no choice but to comply. As I turned, Jax Dunn's disembodied hand slipped into my coat, a grim reminder of the stakes. "What is that?" I asked, startled.

Jax Dunn chuckled, "It's my hand, the one holding the gun."

A chill ran through me. "What is this sorcery?" I demanded.

"I told you, I'm going with you," he replied smugly. "My hand, ever vigilant behind your back. You can't reach it. A person can't bend their arm to touch their own back. That's common sense, isn't it?"

His cold logic was unnerving, and his next words only deepened my sense of doom. "I'll give you one hour. Retrieve the metal sheet and return. One hour, then I shoot."

"One hour is impossible," I protested, my voice edged with desperation. "At least two."

His demands threw my original plan into disarray. I had hoped for leverage, but his conditions left me powerless. "Fine, two hours," he conceded.

I wanted to negotiate further, but he cut me off. "Two hours. Best hurry. Remember, if anything touches my hand or you remove your coat, I fire."

The gun pressed into my arm, a chilling reminder of my vulnerability. I had no choice but to obey.

I made my way to the road, moving quickly. After a tense wait, a streetcar appeared. I boarded, giving the driver the hotel's name. I sat awkwardly, unable to lean back, aware of the hand and gun pressed against me. The driver cast curious glances my way, but I offered no explanation.

Arriving at the hotel, I checked my watch—fifty minutes gone. I had just twenty minutes to act before returning.

How to use these precious minutes?

The clock was ticking, and I needed a plan.

As I spun around the room, precious seconds slipped through my fingers like sand. Ten minutes vanished in a blink—half my time gone. Panic clawed at my thoughts, but then inspiration struck. My hand couldn't reach Jax Dunn's floating hand, but a gun could.

With newfound determination, I took my gun, turned my back to the mirror, and carefully bent my arm, aligning the barrel with the bulge on my back. At such close range, missing was impossible. Yet, a shadow of doubt lingered— would Jax Dunn's hand still fire after being shot? The risk was immense, a gamble more perilous than Russian roulette.

I steadied my nerves, ready to pull the trigger, when a sobering thought hit me—Myles Henry. If I injured Jax Dunn's hand, he might retaliate against Myles Henry. But if I captured the injured hand, preventing its return, Jax Dunn would be forced to negotiate.

Acting on impulse, I sealed the room, locking doors and windows to trap the hand. Then, with a deep breath, I faced the mirror once more and fired.

The silencer muted the shot to a mere "snap." I braced myself, heart pounding. If the hand could still fire, I'd know in a fraction of a second. But if not, I'd see it struggle to escape.

Time stretched painfully as I awaited my fate. Finally, two "bang" sounds echoed, followed by a thud. I turned, confronted by a grotesque sight—a German pistol lay on the floor, and a bloody hand crawled, animated and eerie.

My shot had maimed three fingers, rendering them useless, and I quickly stepped on the gun, securing it. Yet the hand leapt with uncanny vigor, its bloody trail a testament to its determination.

I staggered back, horror gripping me. The hand, relentless, hit the door, its attempt to turn the handle futile. I stood frozen, paralyzed by the macabre spectacle.

With a "clap," the hand hit the floor, scrabbling toward the window. But clarity returned, and I acted. Grabbing a sofa cushion, I hurled it, knocking the hand down before it could reach the glass.

I stripped off my shirt, smothering the hand beneath it. It writhed violently, a grotesque display of defiance. In a moment of absurdity, I found myself shouting, "Don't struggle, don't move," knowing full well the hand couldn't heed my words. Its resistance increased, forcing me to press down harder with my knee. Blood seeped through the fabric, staining my coat and the floor beneath.

Despite its distance from Jax Dunn, the hand moved with intent, controlled by his neural commands. But how could it bleed so profusely? The mystery deepened—how did blood, tangible and finite, transcend the physical separation from its source?

I maintained pressure until the hand's thrashing waned, finally ceasing altogether. Cautiously, I lifted my knee, then my coat, revealing the hand beneath.

It lay in a crimson puddle, unnaturally pale, its life force drained. The absence of further bleeding signaled its defeat. I stood, a maelstrom of emotions churning within. I had aimed to capture a living hand, a potential bargaining chip. Instead, I held a macabre trophy — a dead hand, its absurdity striking.

The very notion of labeling a hand as "alive" or "dead" felt ludicrous, yet here I was, confronting the unimaginable. It was a predicament ripe with panic and existential dread.

As I grappled with these thoughts, a sudden, sharp knock shattered the silence. The sound jolted me, and I instinctively turned to the door, unthinking.

The door flew open, and a man barreled in, a force of nature in his urgency. He shoved past me, driven by unknown motives.

The man lunged toward the floor, his target the "dead hand." Only as he collapsed beside it did I recognize him— Jax Dunn. He clutched the hand with his left, rolling on the ground in a frantic, almost primal dance.

From his throat erupted a sound, a jagged, nerve-grating screech, as if a blade were sawing through the air itself. It was a sound that would unsettle even the steeliest of resolves, sending shivers down anyone's spine.

The scene unfolded with such abruptness and chaos that I barely registered Jax Dunn's movements as he reclaimed the hand. When he finally stopped, the sound ceased, and he stood, his left hand supporting his right. Remarkably, his right hand was reattached, no longer a separate entity but part of his body once more.

The pallor had faded, replaced by a faint, returning flush of blood. We both stood there, stunned, absorbing the bizarre turn of events. As I watched, blood began to trickle from the wound on his right hand. "Mr. Dunn, your hand needs bandaging," I offered, almost instinctively.

But Jax Dunn, driven by fury or desperation, lunged for the German military pistol lying on the floor. I was quicker, pinning it underfoot before delivering a swift punch to his chin.

The impact sent him sprawling, crashing to the ground. Through gritted teeth, he spewed invective, "Son of a bitch, you plague beast..." His face contorted in fury, his words a venomous litany.

I met his gaze, a sneer on my lips. "Jax Dunn, you've failed. You refuse to yield, yet you curse me. That's unwise."

He sprang to his feet, a howl tearing from his throat. "You will regret this. You've pushed me too hard. You will regret it, you will!"

The venom in his eyes, akin to a snake's deadly intent, gave weight to his threats. His words were a chilling promise, and despite my victory, I sensed this was far from over. Jax Dunn's resolve was a coiled serpent, waiting for the moment to strike.

CHAPTER 8

Terrible Accident

I considered compromising with Jax Dunn, but his aggressive demeanor left no room for negotiation. "You're mistaken," I said. "From the start, you've been the one seeking my help, haven't you?"

Had Jax Dunn acknowledged this, the outcome might have been different. But he was as stubborn as a mule, refusing to see the olive branch in my words. Instead, he retorted, "I won't ask you for anything. Never again. I'd rather turn to anyone else than you."

He turned to leave, but I intercepted him. "Where's Myles Henry?"

Panting, Jax Dunn met my gaze. I pressed on, "I just returned your hand to you. I can just as easily take it back.

Tell your people to release Myles Henry and have him return to the hotel. You have two minutes."

The power dynamic had shifted. I was now in control.

Blood dripped from Jax Dunn's wounded hand as he turned and made a call. Speaking in Egyptian, he assumed I couldn't understand, but I picked up enough to know he was arranging Myles Henry's release. Relief washed over me.

When he hung up, silence filled the room, tension crackling between us.

Twenty minutes later, the door swung open, and Myles Henry stepped in, halting at the sight of Jax Dunn. Hesitant, he lingered at the threshold until I reassured him, "Don't worry. Our friend here just experienced a minor setback."

Jax Dunn rose, acknowledging Myles Henry's return with, "Alright, Dr. Henry is back!"

I offered Jax Dunn another chance. "Wouldn't you like to discuss things now?"

True to form, he ignored the opportunity, staggering toward the exit like a drunken man. He paused at the door, casting a disdainful glance back. "You'll regret this. Mark my words—you'll regret it!"

With those parting threats, he stumbled out.

Myles Henry turned to me, eyes darting around the blood-streaked room in disbelief. "What happened? I don't understand. Explain it to me!"

His urgency grated on me. "Can you slow down? First, tell me how Jax Dunn managed to force you out. What happened?"

Myles Henry shook his head, cutting me off. "No, tell me first—do you still have the metal sheet?"

His questions came rapid-fire, leaving me no choice but to recount the bizarre chain of events. As I spoke, the gravity of the situation settled between us, the room bearing silent witness to the chaos that had unfolded.

Myles Henry listened intently as I recounted the surreal events that had unfolded, and then he shared his own ordeal. It was as I suspected: Jax Dunn's hand had forced him out while I was in the shower. Once outside, he was confined in the back of a truck, a hulking guard keeping watch. But then, unexpectedly, someone knocked on the truck, exchanged a few words, and Myles Henry was set free.

With our stories laid bare, Myles Henry mused, "Jax Dunn is desperate for that metal sheet. What secrets could it possibly hold?"

"We need to join forces, Myles Henry," I suggested.

He looked at me, puzzled. "What do you mean?"

"It's simple," I explained, pacing with intent. "We need to decipher the strange inscriptions on the metal sheet. I believe they hold the key to Jax Dunn's secrets."

Myles Henry nodded, seeing the logic. "And what will you do?"

"I'll ensure your work goes undisturbed. Jax Dunn won't give up easily after his loss today. You'll need protection."

Myles Henry seemed to consider objecting, but ultimately he agreed. "Alright, and the metal piece?"

I gestured to the painting. "Still hidden behind it."

With swift efficiency, Myles Henry retrieved the metal sheet from its hiding place and tucked it securely in his coat. "Let's head to the university's graduate school for research. What about you?"

"You should find a private research room," I advised.

Myles Henry agreed that having an independent research room was ideal, but he noted, "I might need help from others during my research. I trust you won't object to that."

I hesitated briefly, weighing the risks. "Just be cautious when choosing your assistants. I'll be stationed outside your research room to ensure security."

We left the hotel and made our way to the university, where Myles Henry's research room awaited on the top floor. It was a spacious area, secluded except for a single entry from the corridor. I conducted a thorough check, ensuring all windows were securely closed, and positioned myself inside by the door.

As Myles Henry delved into the texts, poring over ancient inscriptions, I found myself unable to contribute— his research was highly specialized, far beyond my expertise.

Initially, Myles Henry worked alone, but soon the room filled with scholars, each eager to contribute. Their discussions grew animated, a cacophony of theories and debates. With over a dozen voices competing, I found myself sidelined and somewhat bored, prompting me to step outside for a breath of air.

Standing guard outside the laboratory, I noticed a gathering crowd. Students and onlookers, aware of the scholarly assembly, hovered nearby, pointing and whispering about the mysterious text being studied within. The sheer number of people provided some comfort; Jax Dunn would hesitate to act openly with so many witnesses.

Despite being outside, I could still hear the lively arguments filtering through the door. My vigil continued as I paced back and forth, scanning the corridor.

Soon, three individuals approached, each carrying hefty tomes. Their determined pace suggested urgency. I moved to intercept them. "Who are you?"

The leader, a gaunt man with an air of authority, glared at me. "Step aside. I'm Professor Baker."

His commanding presence nearly made me falter, but I stood firm. "Excuse me, Professor Baker. Professor Myles Henry is conducting research. Have you received his invitation?"

Professor Baker, unfazed, reached out to shove me aside. "Move!"

I wouldn't let Professor Baker simply push past me, so I grasped his arm firmly. In any other situation, I might have been tempted to apply more force, but here, outside a university lab, I needed to be cautious. My restraint was enough to make Baker yelp as if startled by a ghost.

Myles Henry's voice cut through the tension, calling out from the room. "Professor Baker? Come in quickly, I believe this is the last key, waiting for you to explain."

Hearing this, I released my grip, allowing Baker to barge through the door, followed by his two companions. I considered stopping them too, but the previous confrontation made me hesitate. While I dithered, they slipped in behind him.

Left at the door, I found myself under scrutiny from the gathered students, their whispers pricking my awareness. Then, suddenly, an unsettling quiet enveloped the lab.

Moments ago, the room was a hive of activity, filled with debate and discussion. Now, silence pressed against the walls. My instincts screamed that something was amiss. Had they made a breakthrough? If so, there would be cheers, and Myles Henry would have called for me. This silence was ominous.

I rushed to the door, finding it locked. Panic surged as I pounded on it, shouting, but no response came. The urgency of the situation was undeniable. I threw myself against the door, joined by several strong students who had gathered around.

Together, we rammed the door with our shoulders, the wood groaning under our assault until it finally gave way. The scene inside the lab was shocking enough to nearly knock me off my feet.

The room was littered with bodies — scholars and students alike — slumped over chairs or sprawled on the floor. They weren't dead, but unconscious, felled by a potent anesthetic that lingered heavily in the air, its acrid scent clawing at my senses.

I staggered, grasping the doorframe to steady myself. Despite all precautions, disaster had struck.

Rushing inside, I checked each individual, ensuring they were breathing. Relief mingled with frustration. Whoever orchestrated this knew exactly how to incapacitate without causing permanent harm.

I tried to steady myself, scanning the laboratory to assess the situation. My eyes quickly landed on the glaring absence: the metal sheet was missing, and so were the two individuals who had entered with Professor Baker. The sheet had been on the table, under Myles Henry's scrutiny. Now, Myles Henry lay unconscious, still clutching his magnifying glass, but the sheet was gone.

A wave of frustration surged through me. I had been careless, failing to properly vet those two men or even retain a clear image of them. I only recalled their scholarly facade, complete with books tucked under their arms. But given the circumstances, they were likely anything but scholars.

As I stood frozen by the door, voices rose around me, urging, "Call the police, quick! Quick!" Their urgency jolted me, but I felt rooted to the spot, overwhelmed by the realization that Jax Dunn had outmaneuvered us.

Fifteen minutes later, the unconscious scholars were on their way to the hospital. Meanwhile, I found myself at the police station, settled into a small office. The officers treated me with respect, aware of my international police credentials. I used this moment to collect my thoughts, though they were as tangled as ever.

The efficiency with which the two men operated indicated they were professionals. But who were they? And now, with the metal sheet likely in Jax Dunn's hands, what did that mean for us?

My mind was still racing when a middle-aged man entered the room. He moved slowly, his frame heavyset and his hair silvered with age. Yet, his eyes were sharp, suggesting a keen intellect.

He approached, extending a hand. "My name is Ladak. I'm the minister-in-charge of the National Police Agency. I handle all complex cases."

I nodded, still feeling the weight of failure. "I'm Ash Morris."

"We're already aware, Mr. Morris," he assured me. "We're not here to question you, given your international police credentials. We just want to understand what transpired."

I shook my head, frustration evident. "Even if I explain, it may sound unbelievable."

Ladak smiled slightly. "Egypt is a land of ancient mysteries. Here, the incredible is often possible."

His openness encouraged me. Perhaps Ladak was someone I could work with, someone who might understand the nuances of this peculiar situation. If I trusted him, sharing the details could be a step forward.

I sighed, "It's a long story."

Ladak offered a reassuring smile. "You might as well take your time."

Gathering my thoughts, I recounted the intricate tale, including the strange dynamics between myself, Jax Dunn, and Myles Henry, and the bizarre phenomenon of Jax Dunn's limb separation. Ladak listened intently, his face registering a spectrum of emotions, most notably surprise, yet he remained silent until I was finished. His restraint was impressive, a testament to his rational demeanor and ability to suppress curiosity.

After I concluded, Ladak regarded me thoughtfully. "Are you sure everything you said wasn't imagined or an illusion?"

I anticipated this skepticism. Without taking offense, I replied, "I think Myles Henry should have woken by now. You can verify with him."

Ladak sighed, shaking his head, his expression casting a chill over me. Alarmed, I leaned in. "What happened?"

Ladak spoke heavily, "Not only Myles Henry, but all the scholars in that lab... It's a tremendous loss to academia."

My heart sank. "What happened to them? They were knocked out by the anesthetic, right? They didn't wake up?"

"They did wake up," Ladak explained grimly. "But the anesthetic was toxic, destroying their brain nerve tissues. They've become—"

He paused, and I filled the silence, horrified, "Idiots?"

Ladak nodded, his silence confirming the tragedy.

I protested, "How is this possible? The only anesthetic I know of that can cause such damage is a secret weapon used by certain spy agencies. How could anyone else have access to it?"

Ladak sighed, "So, the problem is actually quite simple."

I was taken aback, then realized, "You mean the person who took the metal piece is a spy from some country?"

"That's the only plausible explanation," Ladak affirmed. "Only they would have access to such resources."

I started to suggest, "It might be Jax Dunn—" but stopped, unable to finish.

The implications were staggering. If Jax Dunn was involved with or backed by a powerful spy network, the stakes were much higher than I had imagined. We were dealing with forces far beyond a mere criminal enterprise, potentially entangling us in international espionage. The need to retrieve the metal piece and uncover its secrets had never been more urgent.

As I recalled Jax Dunn's fierce expression and his ominous threats, it struck me that his desperation might have driven him to seek assistance from a foreign spy agency. It was a plausible scenario, given his resourcefulness and the gravity of the situation.

Despite my current frustration, if Jax Dunn indeed allied with a foreign spy network, he could find himself ensnared in a far more dangerous game than he anticipated. Utilizing spies trained in ruthlessness and precision is not a trivial endeavor.

Ladak interrupted my thoughts, asking, "Mr. Morris, do you see the seriousness of the matter?"

I nodded, acknowledging the weight of the situation. Ladak placed a firm hand on my shoulder, stating, "You have no room for refusal. We need your help in this investigation. You must take responsibility in combating them."

His words felt like a heavy burden descending upon me. I wished to avoid it, yet there was no escaping this responsibility. "In reality... this isn't my responsibility," I weakly protested.

Ladak responded firmly, "It is your responsibility, Mr. Morris. Professor Myles Henry is your good friend—do you want him to remain an idiot?"

I retorted, "Can he be saved?"

Ladak replied, "I don't know. Perhaps, perhaps not. But answers will only come if we dismantle their operation and achieve a full victory."

The thought of Myles Henry being permanently affected was a sobering one. I paced, hands clasped behind my back, contemplating the gravity of the situation.

Ladak continued, "Our equipment may be second-rate, but our people are first-rate and ready to follow your lead."

Realizing I could no longer refuse, I stopped pacing and agreed, "Alright, where do we begin?"

Ladak's answer was straightforward. He motioned for me to follow, leading me to a meeting room down the corridor.

Inside, seven or eight people awaited, the atmosphere tense and focused. Upon our entrance, everyone stood.

Ladak introduced me with unexpected reverence, "This is the legendary Mr. Ash Morris. He will lead our efforts. It is our honor."

Flattered by the introduction, I offered a few polite remarks before sitting. Ladak continued, "The enemy's actions have caused significant losses, but we know their base of operations—the embassy of a certain country."

As he spoke, the room darkened, and an image of the embassy appeared on the wall. "Their spies operate from within the embassy, shielded from capture. To be effective, we must infiltrate the embassy."

The slide transitioned to an image of a sewer cover near the embassy. "A journey through the sewer leads to the embassy's cellar. Intelligence suggests this entrance remains unnoticed."

The presentation continued, showing the cellar and a large stone. "Push this stone to access an iron ladder leading to the kitchen," Ladak explained.

Subsequent slides depicted floor plans of the embassy's three levels, though Ladak cautioned, "These plans are seven years old. The internal layout may have changed."

The task ahead was daunting, yet the path was clear. We needed to act swiftly and decisively, leveraging the element of surprise to retrieve the metal sheet and uncover the depths of this conspiracy.

"I understand," I replied. "Are there any reduced drawings of these three plans for me to carry with me?"

"Yes, we will prepare them immediately," he assured.

I pressed on, "What is the main purpose of my mission?"

"The primary goal is to save those scholars. There may be an antidote for the anesthetic," Ladak explained.

"And about Jax Dunn—" I began to ask, but Ladak interrupted firmly, "That is not within the scope of our work, you should understand."

His abruptness caught me off guard. Initially, I was puzzled by his reaction. But the peculiar look he gave me immediately after made things clear. Whether or not he believed my account of Jax Dunn, he wanted to keep this matter under wraps, avoiding any additional complications.

Moreover, I realized that finding an antidote might only be a guise. The true mission lay in uncovering the secrets of Jax Dunn and the metal sheet. Acknowledging this, I nodded, "Yes, I understand."

Ladak addressed the group with gravitas, "Tonight, we will commence the operation. Mr. Morris will infiltrate the embassy of a certain country. He will risk his life to uncover everything within."

He paused, allowing the weight of his statement to settle over the room. The risks were palpable, yet the mission was crucial, not only for the scholars but potentially for international security. The path ahead was fraught with danger, but it was a challenge I was prepared to face.

The tension in the conference room was palpable. Everyone understood the grave risk of infiltrating a foreign embassy. The mission was fraught with danger, and failure meant almost certain death. As such, the room was filled with a mix of admiration and sympathy, with eyes on me as if I were already a ghost walking.

Ladak broke the silence, introducing a special communication device. A man approached, illuminating the room as he opened a velvet box to reveal what appeared to be a tooth. I looked at Ladak, puzzled.

"This," Ladak explained, "is an ultra-short wave radio communication device. Its frequency is unique, minimizing the chance of interception."

I hesitated, "But my teeth are all healthy. There's no room for it."

Ladak reassured me with a smile, "Our country may not be cutting-edge, but our dentists are excellent. Rest assured."

Initially, I was ready to protest further, but I realized the absurdity. In a mission with life-and-death stakes, worrying about a tooth seemed trivial. I conceded, "Alright, how does it work?"

Ladak explained, "Simple. Once fitted, it's in your upper jaw. Tap your jaws to send a signal. You can use coded messages, even Morse code."

I tried to lighten the mood with, "I'll have to be careful when I eat." But my attempt at humor fell flat in the somber room, and I quickly stopped.

Ladak continued, "We've scheduled your dental appointment for post-meeting. We also have self-defense weapons for you to consider."

Another officer presented a box containing various small weapons. The ingenuity in these tools was both fascinating and unsettling, reflecting humanity's paradoxical advancement in weaponry over medicine. Even as common ailments like the cold persisted, our ability to devise means of destruction had progressed to staggering levels.

Within the box, no hydrogen bombs, of course, but an array of lethal gadgets lay before me. After careful consideration, I selected three.

Among them was a fake fingertip, designed to fit over the middle finger of my right hand. This seemingly innocuous prosthetic concealed seven poison needles, capable of firing instantly and lethally within a five-step range.

The gravity of the mission ahead was underscored by these preparations. It was clear that I was being equipped for a perilous journey, one that required both cunning and courage to navigate the treacherous path to uncover the secrets of the embassy and the truth behind Jax Dunn's machinations.

CHAPTER 9

Escape in the Embassy

The second item I selected was a belt buckle with a unique function. When pressed, it emitted a terrifying, piercing sound capable of stunning anyone for several seconds, regardless of their fortitude. In an emergency, this could be the edge needed to shift the balance in my favor.

The third weapon was a compact pistol. Despite its small size, it packed a significant punch. Though it appeared to use regular bullets, these were actually potent mini-explosives. The officer informed me that firing all seven "bullets" simultaneously could level the entire embassy.

After selecting my weapons, I was whisked away to a highly skilled dentist. With surprising ease and no pain, he extracted one of my molars and replaced it with the communication device.

Once the anesthetic wore off, a dull ache set in, and I took a few hours to rest. When I awoke, night had fallen.

Gathering my resolve, I met with Ladak and proceeded to a house situated opposite the embassy. From this vantage point, I had a clear view of the manhole cover — the entrance to my clandestine route.

The embassy's windows glowed with light, though thick curtains obscured any view inside.

Following Ladak's radio command, a large man appeared, nonchalantly approaching the manhole. With a hooked cane, he deftly lifted the cover about half a foot before continuing on as if nothing were amiss.

His nonchalance was crucial, allowing me to reach the manhole unnoticed and slip beneath it without any delay, minimizing the risk of detection.

If the embassy suspected anything about the manhole, the man's actions would likely draw their attention, possibly prompting them to investigate and forcing me to adjust my plans.

After he left, I waited a tense half-hour, watching for any signs of movement. The street remained silent.

I exited the house, fully equipped with my gear. Clad in rubber waterproof clothing and carrying an oxygen mask, I was prepared for the sewer's challenges.

I dashed across the street to the manhole, lowering myself down and carefully replacing the cover to avoid noise, completing the maneuver in less than thirty seconds.

The initial descent was straightforward, aided by an iron ladder. My flashlight illuminated the path below, casting a grim, gray-black glow on the sluggish sewage and releasing a vile stench.

Immersing my lower body in the sewage, I shuddered at the methane bubbles rising from the depths. Despite the protective gear, the sensation was unsettling.

I advanced cautiously, aware that a misstep could have dire consequences. After about ten steps, I reached a bend where the sewage shallowed, easing my progress slightly. The journey was just beginning, and I steeled myself for the challenges ahead, intent on reaching my destination within the embassy's depths.

As I continued, I eventually spotted the red cross sign that Ladak had described. This marked the location of the movable stone. Pushing it forward would grant me access to the embassy's cellar.

Approaching with caution, I affixed a small micro-amplifier to the stone, listening intently for any sounds from the other side. The last thing I needed was to stumble upon someone unexpectedly in the cellar. After a long, tense moment, silence reassured me that the coast was clear.

Pushing the stone proved more difficult than anticipated. It required all my strength, and I nearly lost my footing several times. Once it started moving, however, the task became easier. Eventually, I managed to slip through the gap into the cellar.

The cellar was enveloped in darkness. As I switched on my flashlight, its beam caught countless tiny, reflective dots darting around—rat eyes. While unpleasant, the presence of so many rats was a relief. Their numbers indicated that the cellar had been undisturbed for some time, allowing me the chance to proceed without immediate threat.

I quickly shed my soiled rubber clothing, repositioned the stone to conceal my entrance, and surveyed the cellar. It was surprisingly spacious. My first task was to set up a precautionary measure: I attached a special "bullet" equipped with a small radio induction device to the cellar wall. This setup meant that with a press of my ring, I could remotely detonate the explosive if necessary.

With that done, I turned my attention to the iron ladder leading upward. According to Ladak, it should lead to the embassy's kitchen. Yet, as I examined the ladder, I noticed that the door at the top appeared to have been unused for quite some time. Dust and cobwebs suggested that this was not a frequently traveled path, contradicting the information I had been given.

This discrepancy made me pause. If the cellar was not directly connected to the kitchen as expected, it meant I needed to reassess my approach and remain vigilant for any surprises. Carefully, I began to climb the ladder, ready to adapt to whatever lay beyond the door at its summit.

Hearing nothing, I decided to proceed carefully. Peering through a crack beneath the door, I saw only dim light, confirming that it wasn't the kitchen outside. This was a relief. If it led directly into a busy kitchen, my presence would be more easily detected.

I took out a sharp knife and began to work on the door, carefully carving out a hole to remove the lock. Once the lock fell off, I quietly opened the door to find a large room filled with miscellaneous items—a storage room. This was ideal, as it provided a buffer zone, reducing the chance of immediate discovery.

I moved to the door of the storage room, listening again. This time, I detected a faint "squeaking" sound, likely the noise of leather shoes on carpet, indicating someone was nearby. I waited until the sound faded, then used a small periscope through the keyhole to survey the corridor outside. The view was limited, but I could make out a large oak door at one end of the corridor and a staircase at the other.

Comparing this with the outdated embassy plans, it was clear that the interior layout had changed significantly. What was supposed to be a workshop and a small corridor was now entirely different. This realization underscored the unpredictability of the mission.

Retracting the periscope, I prepared to leave the storage room, planning to hide in a small room under the stairs. With a lily key, I hoped to unlock the door in about 20 seconds, allowing me to officially enter the embassy undetected.

Quietly opening the storage room door, I dashed to the small room under the stairs and began working on the lock with the lily key. However, my expectations were quickly dashed as the lock refused to yield. Despite my skill, a full minute passed without success, leaving me exposed as voices approached from the other side of the oak door.

I retreated back to the storage room, closing the door behind me and using the periscope to watch. Two individuals emerged from the oak door, one of whom I recognized as having accompanied Professor Baker into the lab. They moved up the stairs, their presence confirming my suspicions of espionage.

Once their footsteps faded, I attempted the small room's lock again. This time, it took a painstaking three minute. Despite my efforts, I was unable to unlock the small door. Suddenly, I heard three distinct "clicks" from within the room — unmistakably the sound of machine gears shifting. This was peculiar for what should have been a simple storeroom under the stairs. Alarmed, I instinctively stepped back.

As I retreated, I noticed the door handle turning. Someone was about to emerge from the room! It was an unexpected and incredible turn of events. There was no time to retreat to the storage room; the door swung open, and a figure stooped low as they exited, straightening up to find themselves face-to-face with me.

The surprise etched on the man's face mirrored my own. We were both caught off guard, but I had a slight advantage. My initial shock had peaked when I saw the door handle turn, giving me a crucial moment to regain composure.

In contrast, his alarm reached its zenith upon seeing me—a stranger standing unexpectedly before him. In that split second, I acted. With a swift horizontal turn of my elbow, I struck his chest forcefully. It was a potentially lethal blow, but in such a critical situation, I had no choice.

The man crumpled silently against me, save for the dull thud of the impact. I quickly maneuvered his falling body, dragging him into the small room and closing the door behind us to avoid immediate detection.

Inside the room, I knew my safety was temporary; the possibility of another person emerging was real.

I switched on my flashlight, and what I saw left me stunned.

The small room was impeccably clean, and to my surprise, there was an iron door where a wall should have been. It was the first door to a secret room, and I realized that my choice of hiding place had serendipitously led me to this discovery.

I dragged the now lifeless man to the corner and placed him there. His unfortunate fate left me with a dilemma: I needed to open the iron door, but it was perfectly smooth with no visible handles or locks. Using my flashlight, I found no obvious way to open it, confirming that it was likely radio-controlled. I searched the man's pockets and found a flat box with several buttons of different colors — a radio controller.

Despite having the controller, I hesitated. Seven buttons meant seven potential outcomes, but which one controlled the iron door? The risk of pressing the wrong button was high, leaving me with only a one in seven chance of success. Momentarily, I regretted my earlier actions, as the man could have provided the information I needed.

With no immediate solution, I decided to wait and see if anyone would emerge from the iron door. I crouched in the corner, ready to spring into action like a predator in the shadows. After about half an hour, I heard a familiar "click" and watched as the iron door rose, contrary to my expectations.

A man stepped out, oblivious to my presence, and moved towards the small door's handle. Seizing the moment, I leapt forward, silently yet swiftly. He was startled, and as he began to turn, I was already upon him, securing his head and neck in a tight grip while pressing my gun against his forehead.

"Don't move, don't make a sound," I whispered. His brief struggle ceased, and I loosened my hold slightly to let him breathe. "Listen," I continued softly, "I want you to obey me completely."

He nodded, and I pressed on, "First, take me through this iron gate. The real nerve center of your operations is inside, right?"

"It's useless," he muttered, "It's useless for you to go in."

"Don't worry about that," I insisted. "The person in charge here isn't the ambassador, is it?"

He remained silent, prompting my suspicion. I guessed, "You're the one in charge here, aren't you?"

His body betrayed him with a slight shiver, confirming my suspicions. I had indeed captured the leader of this operation.

"Then let's make this easy," I said with a grin. "Take me to your office, and we can discuss further."

Reluctantly, he retrieved a radio control device from his pocket and pressed a button, causing the iron door to rise again. What lay beyond was beyond anything I could have imagined. My initial triumph at capturing the leader was suddenly overshadowed by the unexpected scene before me, leaving me on the brink of disbelief.

The moment the iron door rose, I was blinded by a bright light that left me momentarily disoriented. As my eyes adjusted, the gravity of the situation became clear: seven or eight large men, each armed with portable machine guns, stood ready, weapons trained directly on me.

I hadn't turned my back after subduing the man, so I quickly maneuvered him in front of me as a human shield. My only hope was that this man was indeed the leader, preventing his subordinates from firing indiscriminately.

Their initial panic and the slight droop of their gun muzzles indicated my assumption might be correct. I felt a fleeting sense of triumph, but it was short-lived. With a sudden "bang," the small door behind me burst open.

Instantly, I felt the cold press of gun muzzles against my head, back, and waist. Commands were barked at me from behind: "Let go of the man, raise your hands, and drop the pistol!"

Instinctively, I almost complied, caught between two armed groups. But in a split second, I realized I couldn't release my hold on the man. If he was the leader, maintaining control over him was my leverage.

The weapons behind me were powerful; any shot fired would penetrate us both. I took a deep breath, steadying myself. Turning slightly, I saw five more armed individuals behind me, their guns mere inches from my head.

Addressing them coldly, I said, "I suggest you lower your weapons. A single bullet could easily take out two people here. You don't want that, do you?"

Faced with my ultimatum, the group behind me hesitated, visibly uneasy. I tapped the forehead of my captive with my pistol, "Isn't that right?" I pressed, ensuring my point was clear.

The man I held was immobilized, my arm locked around his neck, knee against his waist. My thumb pressed into his neck, eliciting a pained groan. As his cries peaked, I loosened my grip slightly.

"You gathered these people," I said, addressing him directly. "You know how to handle this situation."

The man growled defiantly, "If you don't let me go, they'll shoot you dead!" Despite the dire situation, I couldn't help but chuckle, though the laughter came out forced and unnatural. "Sure, they might shoot me," I replied, "but you know your fate will be sealed too."

His defiance gave way to a violent struggle, but I tightened my grip, maintaining control. After about a minute, he relented, instructing his men to back off. The armed figures retreated, though I was under no illusion that the threat had vanished. They were simply repositioning out of sight, likely with weapons still trained on me.

"Is that enough?" the man asked, a hint of impatience in his voice.

"Far from it," I replied, taking a moment to assess my surroundings. The room beyond the iron door was a large conference room, centered around a long table, now empty.

"What else do you want?" he demanded.

"To your office," I insisted. I needed a private space for negotiation, free from prying eyes and ears. His office, I assumed, would be secure and private, befitting a leader's workspace.

He hesitated, realizing the implications. "Too much, that's too much," he protested.

"Not at all," I countered. "Will you take me there?"

His posture stiffened, and after a moment of silence, he complied. We moved through the conference room, navigating a passageway, ascending a spiral staircase, and traversing a hallway until we reached a door. With a frustrated kick, he opened it. "This is it!" he announced angrily.

I glanced inside, taking in the opulent and spacious office. "Very good," I said, satisfied. "Now, let's negotiate. First, have your men return the metal piece they stole from the university lab."

With my arm still locked around his neck, his voice was muffled and defensive. "What metal piece? I don't know anything about it."

I pressed on, "If you're going to act, I can start by shooting you in the ear. Maybe that'll make your performance more convincing."

He winced, understanding my seriousness. "Then you have to let me go first," he conceded.

I weighed my options and decided to release my grip, knowing I still had the upper hand with the gun in hand. "Just remember," I warned, "any tricks, and you'll regret it."

As I released him, I delivered a swift kick to his backside, sending him sprawling to the floor. He quickly recovered, glaring at me with a mix of anger and pain etched across his twisted features.

With a steady hand, I gestured with the gun. "Now, tell your men to bring the metal piece."

He moved towards the desk, but I anticipated trouble and fired a warning shot, skimming his cheek and embedding into the wall behind him. A thin line of blood appeared where the bullet had passed, and he froze in place, shocked.

"What is this?" he demanded, his voice shaking with fury.

I smirked, twirling the gun casually. "Consider it a reminder that my aim is precise, and any sudden moves might be your last."

He stood there, the blood trickling down unchecked as he evaluated his options. After a tense moment, he walked to the desk, pressed a button on the intercom, and said, "Number 7, bring the spoils of Operation Eagle to my office."

The cryptic phrase piqued my curiosity. "What do you mean by 'spoils of Operation Eagle'?" I asked sharply.

He responded coldly, "It's what you came for." I sensed a trap, so I issued another warning, "If you're planning anything—"

Before I could finish, he spread his hands defensively. "What can I do? You're the one with the gun, right?"

I didn't trust his sudden compliance, so I acted decisively. In one swift motion, I twisted his arm behind him and placed the gun against his back, ensuring he stayed under control.

Despite regaining the upper hand, I remained cautious. I was still deep within their territory, and his cryptic language left me uneasy. Moments later, a knock at the door interrupted us.

"Come in," the man said calmly.

The door opened, and a man entered with his head down, carrying a flat briefcase. Without looking up, he placed it on the table. "The spoils of Operation Eagle," he announced before retreating and closing the door behind him.

"There's what you want," the man said, nodding towards the briefcase.

I eyed the case, its size suggesting it could indeed contain the metal piece. However, the repeated mention of "Operation Eagle" fueled my suspicions. I released his arm, shoving him towards the table. "Open it," I demanded. "Let me see."

As soon as I released his hand, I gave him another shove, positioning him next to the table. His reaction was immediate and unexpected—he jumped back as if the briefcase housed a nest of rattlesnakes, panting heavily and clearly signaling that it was untouchable.

I smirked, brandishing my gun. "Seems like you won't cooperate until I take an ear off."

He waved his hands frantically. "No, no, the item you want is indeed in the briefcase!"

"Then take it out for me," I demanded.

He sighed, "I can't. You don't understand, I can't."

"Of course," I retorted. "Because opening it spells certain death, right?"

He quickly denied, "No, it's not that."

"Do you think pretending to be pitiful will save you?" I pressed on. "Do you really think I'll buy it?"

"You don't have to believe me," he insisted. "The metal piece belongs to someone with... unusual powers. He warned me not to touch it. Only his men are allowed to handle it until he retrieves it."

"And what did you get in return?" I asked.

"A big reward."

"Hmph, a personal gain at the expense of your country's resources. Using spies for your profit. What would your superiors say?"

His face paled at the implication.

"Don't worry," I continued, raising my gun. "The metal piece holds no such mysterious power. Open the briefcase, and we'll see you did nothing wrong."

He hesitated but finally approached the briefcase. Just as he reached out to open it, chaos erupted.

Two hands — Jax Dunn's hands, evident from the scars — materialized from nowhere. One snatched the briefcase, while the other flung open the door.

I lunged forward, shouting in anger. The briefcase was within reach, but the spy chief blindsided me, ramming into me sideways. I twisted to avoid the brunt of his attack, delivering a swift kick to his lower abdomen. He cried out, collapsing backward, likely destined for a hospital stay.

Yet, even if my kick incapacitated him for life, it was meaningless now. Jax Dunn and the briefcase were gone.

I sprinted to the door, but the corridor beyond was empty, my pursuit thwarted. The metal piece — and whatever secrets it held—had slipped through my fingers once more.

CHAPTER 10

The Death of
the Fragmented Man

I slammed the door shut and turned back to the man on the floor, yanking him to his feet. His face contorted in pain, and he groaned wretchedly. Ignoring his discomfort, I shook him and shouted, "Stop playing dead. We have unfinished business!"

Finally, through clenched teeth, he managed to ask, "What... what's the matter?"

I let out a cold laugh. "The pain you're feeling now? It's just the beginning. If you refuse my next request, you'll regret it even more."

His silence spoke volumes.

"I won't lay another finger on you," I continued. "But I will inform your superiors of your actions."

At that, he trembled more than any physical blow could have caused. "Just tell me what you want," he pleaded.

I nodded. "Good. To get that metal piece, you drugged six scholars with strong anesthetics. Do you realize what that can do? It can completely shut down their brain functions."

"I know, I know," he muttered, his fear palpable.

"Then give me the antidote," I demanded.

His face fell. "There is no antidote. It's not that I'm withholding it—there truly isn't one."

Rage surged through me. "No antidote? You dared to use such a dangerous substance on innocent people?"

He flinched at my anger. "I... I had no choice. The metal piece promised me wealth beyond imagination. I could finally stop being a spy!"

His desperation was genuine. Yet, the thought of Myles Henry potentially becoming brain-dead was devastating. I gripped the man's shirt, my hand trembling with a mix of anger and helplessness. After a moment, I let him go, watching him crumble to the floor.

Despite infiltrating the embassy and capturing the spy chief, Jax Dunn had ultimately won. He had the metal piece, and Myles Henry's fate was sealed. It felt like a crushing defeat.

I stared at the man for a long time before asking, "If you got the metal piece, how were you supposed to deliver it to Jax Dunn?"

"I was to take it to Kuala Lumpur," he replied. "Jax Dunn would sign over several industries to me, and I'd hand over the metal piece. It was a fair trade."

I realized Jax Dunn had offered him the same deal he proposed to me.

Despite Jax Dunn's promises of immense wealth, they had no allure for me. But clearly, they had enticed the spy chief, who now found himself with nothing, while Jax Dunn emerged victorious with the prized metal sheet.

I was left with more questions than answers about Jax Dunn and the secrets of the metal sheet. The thought of returning to face Ladakh empty-handed was daunting, but neither could I linger in the embassy indefinitely.

Resigned, I asked the spy chief, "You're not planning on going to Kuala Lumpur now, are you?"

He replied bitterly, "Why would I? It's all over now."

I intended to have him escort me out, but a thought struck me. "Your identity is highly confidential. How did Jax Dunn make contact with you?"

He hesitated before admitting, "I've handled similar dealings before. A contact person approached me. It's somewhat known, not entirely secret."

I pressed further, "And this informant—what's his name and where can I find him?"

He answered, "His name is Yaba. Every day at 3 PM, he's at a park on the city's outskirts, under a stone statue, regardless of the weather."

While the lead was tenuous, it was my only potential link to Jax Dunn. I decided to pursue it. I hoisted the spy chief up and instructed, "You're going to ensure I leave here through the main gate."

I discreetly tapped the radio transmitter tucked in my jaw, signaling Ladakh to have a car ready at a nearby embassy's main gate.

With the spy chief at gunpoint, we made our way out. Thanks to my control over him, our departure was unhindered, yet it felt like a hollow victory given the circumstances.

As we exited, a car sped towards us. Ladakh was behind the wheel, and as he pulled up, the door swung open. I shoved the spy chief to the ground and leapt into the vehicle.

Once inside, I didn't bother shutting the door immediately. Instead, I turned and fired twice at the spy chief's knees. His screams echoed as he writhed on the pavement, and with that, Ladakh gunned the engine, and we sped away.

My actions against the spy chief were driven by pure indignation. Myles Henry and the other scholars had been subjected to such cruel and shameless methods, and my anger compelled me to ensure the spy chief would pay a lasting price. By shooting him in the knees, I knew he'd face a permanent disability.

As Ladakh and I drove away, the silence lingered until he broke it with a simple question: "Why?"

"Because there was no antidote," I replied, frustration evident in my voice.

Ladakh sighed, already anticipating the response. "And the metal piece?"

"Jax Dunn took it," I admitted, my voice tinged with defeat.

His bitter smile mirrored my feelings. "Mr. Morris, it might be best for you to leave here soon."

But I shook my head, resolute. "No, there's still a lead, however slim. I'm not giving up yet."

"What lead?" Ladakh inquired.

"The spy chief has a contact, Yaba. He appears in a suburban park every afternoon. I need to find him," I explained.

Ladakh nodded, pulling the car to a stop. I was unsure of our location and puzzled by the sudden halt.

Before I could question him, Ladakh spoke, "Our involvement in this matter has put the police in a difficult position. If word gets out that we relied on you and you failed, the backlash will be severe. From now on, it's best if you have no ties to us."

I was momentarily stunned. "I understand," I replied, though resentment simmered beneath my calm exterior. When they needed me, I was a hero. Now that I had failed, they were discarding me. I had never been used so blatantly before. "Do you want me to get out now?" I asked coldly.

Ladakh's embarrassed smile said it all. Without waiting for an answer, I exited the car. "Mr. Ladakh, remember, we have no ties," I declared, making a cutting gesture with my hand.

He tried to justify, "You must be blaming us—"

I ignored him, striding away angrily. After two blocks, my anger subsided enough to think clearly.

I had one path left: find Yaba. Flagging a taxi, I directed the driver to the park on the city's outskirts. Thirty minutes later, I arrived.

The park was little more than an open space dotted with trees. I found a bench near the statue and sat down, checking my watch. It was still early, and though exhausted from the night's events, sleep eluded me. My mind was too cluttered with thoughts of the embassy, Jax Dunn, and the elusive secrets of the metal piece.

Unable to sleep, I got up and paced the park, trying to clear my mind. The sparse crowd made it an ideal spot for clandestine meetings — a smart choice by Yaba for his dealings with the embassy's spy chief.

Time crawled by, but finally, at 2:50, I spotted a heavyset man approaching slowly. At precisely 3:00, he sat on the bench near the stone statue. This was undoubtedly Yaba.

I approached him, not expecting much. If Jax Dunn had already reached out to him, what could I possibly glean from this encounter?

As I neared, Yaba looked up, and suddenly, the atmosphere shifted. His demeanor changed abruptly—he straightened, reaching back with a hand that grasped at nothing. His face contorted in pain and confusion, eyes wide with disbelief.

I was as bewildered as he was, but quickly realized Yaba had been attacked from behind. He was dying, yet no one stood behind him. This could only mean one thing: Jax Dunn's notorious hands had struck again.

There was no gunshot, and Yaba's condition didn't suggest a bullet wound. It had to be a stabbing. Jax Dunn's hand must have been lurking nearby, waiting to strike at 3:00 sharp.

Pulling a knife from a person's back isn't easy, and since I hadn't seen any hand retreat, it was likely still there, gripping the weapon.

Acting on instinct, I lunged forward, pressing Yaba against the bench. He wasn't dead yet, his eyes bulging as he made a horrible, gurgling gasp—an unsettling sound of blood choking his throat.

Despite the repulsive noise, I held him down, searching desperately for any sign of Jax Dunn's hidden assailant. This was my chance—perhaps my only chance—to turn the tide and discover what Jax Dunn was hiding.

Once I pressed Yaba down, I realized that Jax Dunn's hand was likely trapped between Yaba's body and the bench.

I couldn't afford to relax my hold, not while there was still a chance to capture Jax Dunn's elusive hand. Luckily, the park was deserted, sparing me from unwanted attention as I lay atop a dying man—a situation that would surely raise alarms if witnessed.

As the choking sounds from Yaba's throat subsided, I felt an unexpected resistance from beneath him. His chest heaved, but not with his own breath; something beneath was straining against him. It was Jax Dunn's hand, struggling to free itself! This was my opportunity to regain control over the situation.

My hand cautiously slipped around Yaba's body, reaching behind him until I felt the unmistakable presence of Jax Dunn's hand. Grasping a finger, I twisted it forcefully until I heard a satisfying "snap," rendering the hand powerless.

With that assurance, I pushed Yaba's body aside. Though the hand's remaining fingers clawed at me, I endured the pain and sprinted away, maintaining my grip on the captured finger. After covering a good distance, I stopped and stomped on the hand, hearing its bones crack underfoot.

True to form, Jax Dunn appeared, sweating and breathless, rushing towards me. He paused briefly before diving to the ground, desperately reconnecting his severed hand to his wrist. Before he could fully recover, I seized the moment, delivering a powerful kick to his face.

The impact was brutal, sending Jax Dunn reeling. Though his body tilted backward, his hand remained pinned under my foot, causing his arm to emit an awful "click" as he fell.

Taking advantage of his stunned state, I hauled him up by his clothes, slinging one of his arms over my shoulder. He was unconscious, allowing me to drag him out of the park without a fuss. Outside, I found his abandoned car, the door left ajar.

I shoved him into the backseat, ensuring he was secure. To prevent any chance of him waking during the journey, I delivered a firm punch to the back of his head, knocking him out cold. Now, with Jax Dunn in my custody, the tables had turned, and I had the chance to uncover the secrets he had so desperately tried to protect.

I stuffed Jax Dunn into the car, ensuring he remained unconscious with a firm punch to the back of his head. As I drove through unfamiliar streets, I kept my distance from Myles Henry's hospital and his heavily guarded residence. I wanted no further entanglements with the police.

Eventually, I stopped in a desolate area. Jax Dunn was still out cold, so I hoisted him up and shook him vigorously, double-checking his body for any signs of detachment at his head, neck, or wrists. To my surprise, there were none—he appeared completely ordinary.

After about ten minutes, Jax Dunn began to groan, slowly regaining consciousness. I stopped shaking him and let him come to. When he finally cracked his eyes open, they were red and swollen from my earlier kick.

"It's you again! It's you again!" he groaned, recognizing me.

"Yes, it's me again," I replied, my tone icy.

"What a pity, what a pity," Jax Dunn muttered.

I grabbed his chest, demanding, "What's a pity?"

His response caught me off guard. "If you give me another 24 hours, humph, ten Ashes would also turn to ashes in my hands!"

His words were chilling. Despite his repeated failures against me, Jax Dunn's threats often came true, and I couldn't dismiss them lightly.

Feigning disdain, I retorted, "In another 24 hours, will you become invincible?"

Jax Dunn grew agitated. "In another 24 hours, I, I, I will—" he faltered, seemingly realizing he'd said too much and abruptly fell silent.

I sensed he was harboring a crucial secret, perhaps baiting me with it. But my thoughts were on Myles Henry, my friend whose mind Jax Dunn had destroyed. Revenge was my only focus now.

"You'll reap what you've sown with your cruel methods," I sneered.

Jax Dunn merely glared at me, offering no rebuttal. Fueled by anger and the need for justice, I grabbed his shirt again and slapped him hard across the face twice, leaving bloody marks at the corners of his mouth and vivid handprints on his cheeks.

The two handprints on Jax Dunn's face turned from white to red as he whimpered, pleading for mercy. "Don't hit me, I've told you, don't hit me!"

I leaned in, my voice fierce with anger. "Don't hit you? Do you realize that your actions have turned six brilliant scholars into mindless shells? Do you understand the gravity of your crimes? Not only will I hit you, but I'll keep hitting you until you experience the same fate."

With that, I delivered another harsh slap. Jax Dunn's hands flailed weakly, "Don't hit me! Don't hit me!"

But then, something inexplicable happened. His expression shifted, and his facial muscles contorted grotesquely. Suddenly, his head detached from his neck in a shocking, surreal moment that defied all logical understanding. I was holding a living body, yet his head floated away, laughing maniacally.

Startled and filled with dread, I released my grip. Jax Dunn's body, now headless, sprang up, opened the car door, and fled. The head and body merged seamlessly outside the car, a spectacle both terrifying and infuriating.

Fueled by rage, I revved the engine and pursued him without a second thought. The car barreled toward Jax Dunn, and as he turned to face his fate, horror etched across his features, he screamed—a sound lost beneath the roar of the engine.

The impact sent him flying, and I slammed the brakes, my initial anger giving way to regret. I hurried over to where he lay, knowing I had gone too far.

Jax Dunn was gravely injured, beyond saving even if medical help arrived immediately. Blood oozed from his mouth, yet he struggled to speak.

I bent closer, urging him, "If you have anything to say, say it now!"

His lips quivered, "Are you... satisfied?"

Any remorse I felt evaporated at his words. I retorted coldly, "Even your death can't restore the scholars. How can I be satisfied?"

To my astonishment, a cunning smile spread across Jax Dunn's swollen face—a look that seemed impossible for someone on the brink of death. "Yes, I can make them sober. There's nothing impossible... If I have that power, I can do everything... I have... everything... power..."

Disbelief mingled with hope. "You mean the six scholars can be restored?"

Jax Dunn struggled to nod, confirming, "Yes!"

But then he collapsed again, whispering his final words with spite, "But I... will never tell you!"

The venom in his voice was unforgettable. I realized any further questioning was futile. This was his ultimate revenge—taking the secret to his grave.

I stood there, stunned. Within minutes, Jax Dunn exhaled his last breath, and life left his body. His face transformed, becoming grotesque in death, and I turned away, unable to look.

Yet, his words ignited a flicker of hope. If there was a way to save Myles Henry and the others, I had to find it. Jax Dunn's hatred had convinced me of the truth in his claim.

Determined to find a way to save the six scholars, I knew I couldn't wander aimlessly. The best chance for clues lay with Jax Dunn, so I stayed behind to search his belongings.

Turning back to his body, I rifled through his pockets and discovered a notebook, a wallet, and assorted odds and ends. In the wallet, a stack of business cards caught my attention. They bore the name "Jie Dunn," with the title "Head of an Archaeological Group"—a title befitting Egypt's archaeological interests—and an address. Despite the alias, I was certain it was another identity used by Jax Dunn.

Remembering Professor Young's mention of Jax Dunn's multiple aliases at the dance party, I surmised that this address must be his residence. With Jax Dunn dead, unraveling the mysteries of his life was now even more difficult, but his home could hold vital clues. He had claimed to know a way to restore Myles Henry and the others. If any hints remained, they would be there.

I returned to the car, leaving Jax Dunn's body behind in the wilderness. Someone would eventually find him and classify him as an unidentified body. I had no patience left to dwell on him further.

My encounters with Jax Dunn had marked some of the most unpleasant days of my life, culminating in the regrettable act of striking him with my car in a fit of rage. Though he had been a despicable figure, the memory of taking a life in anger was deeply unsettling. Coupled with the scholars' tragic fate and the mystery of Jax Dunn's bizarre abilities, my frustration was palpable. I blamed Jax Dunn for this turmoil and left his body behind, driving for miles until my irritation began to fade.

Entering the city, I faced the challenge of locating the address. I asked police officers along the way and, while driving at a moderate pace, took the opportunity to peruse the notebook.

The pages were filled with routine notes. Recent entries mentioned "meeting with Yaba" and "negotiating terms with No. 1," whom I assumed was the spy chief I'd incapacitated. On the day of the laboratory incident, Jax Dunn had written "bless me," followed by blank pages.

The notebook offered little insight, but I found several six-digit numbers scribbled in the back. They could be combinations for a safe—perhaps important.

After asking around, I finally arrived at a small gray house, its British architectural style hinting at its past occupants. The house was eerily quiet, seemingly uninhabited, but I rang the doorbell anyway.

After waiting five minutes with no response, I used the master key to unlock the door and stepped inside. The house was silent, and the air carried a musty scent, as though it hadn't been disturbed for some time. If there were answers to be found, they were hidden within these walls, and I was determined to uncover them.

CHAPTER 11

Jax Dunn's Diary

The interior of Jax Dunn's house was shrouded in darkness, casting an eerie, unsettling feeling over me as I stepped inside. The dim light and fully drawn curtains only added to the sense of being deceived or treated unfairly, as though the house was a facade hiding deeper mysteries.

The British-style layout featured stairs and a corridor leading to the kitchen, with the living room branching off to the side. Despite its outward charm, the house felt unwelcoming.

I cautiously explored the downstairs area but found nothing unusual, prompting me to head upstairs to investigate the five rooms there. Opening the first door, I was taken aback by what I saw.

The room reminded me of a glimpse I'd once had of one of Jax Dunn's bedrooms. It contained nothing but a large box in the center, much like a coffin. The box was closed, and against the walls were strange, indescribable objects resembling instruments. However, these weren't modern but antiquated, like relics from another era.

These instruments were mounted on rough, irregular stones, adorned with indecipherable symbols and pointers. Metal wires snaked out from these devices towards the box in the center. When I opened the box, I found it empty. Yet, a powerful compulsion urged me to climb inside, to lie down just as I had seen Jax Dunn do.

Resisting the urge, I felt a sudden wave of terror wash over me—a chilling sensation that made my skin crawl and my scalp tingle. Hastily, I left the room, feeling as though I had narrowly escaped a sinister fate.

Lingering at the door, still shaken, I resolved not to re-enter that room. Instead, I moved to the second room, which was reminiscent of another space I had seen in Jax Dunn's residence. The walls featured grooves perfectly shaped to hold various human body parts, and in the center stood a peculiar chair woven with ropes and supported by dark, black wood.

The third room, however, appeared normal. A study, it housed a messy desk, two rows of bookcases, and a couple of armchairs. As I approached the desk, I noticed it was cluttered with papers. Beneath them lay the metal plate—the very plate that had been the focus of the scholars' research and the cause of so much chaos.

Under the plate was a piece of paper with four lines of English, written in a staggered fashion that suggested they had been translated laboriously, word by word, over time. The differences in ink and the lack of fluidity between the words confirmed this.

The translation read:

"The high priest of the Bertre Dynasty is the incarnation of the bull god. He has the ability to bring people back to life. His tomb is underground ten miles east of the great Zeus Temple. All his powers went to his tomb with his death. The high priest is the incarnation of God. Countless people can confirm this. The high priest———"

The translation ended abruptly, with Jax Dunn having only managed to decipher a fraction of the text on the metal sheet. His mark indicated the last word he worked on, but it seemed he had barely scratched the surface.

Initially, the translation didn't seem significant. Claims of divine incarnation were common in ancient Egyptian artifacts, and the idea of worshiping someone as a god persisted in various cultures, even into the modern era. My skepticism about the metal sheet's value grew. Why had Jax Dunn gone to such lengths to obtain it, ultimately leading to his demise in the wilderness?

I set aside the metal sheet and the paper, retreating to an armchair to think. Despite reaching Jax Dunn's residence, I felt no closer to a solution. Was there truly no hope for Myles Henry and the others? Could their condition never be reversed?

As I sat there, my mind raced in circles until a sudden realization struck me. The discrepancy in the house's layout suggested a hidden secret. The second floor was significantly larger than the downstairs area — an architectural impossibility unless there was a concealed room.

Excited by the prospect, I hurried back downstairs and began to search meticulously. Within 20 minutes, I uncovered a hidden feature: two sets of dials embedded in the wall behind a large oil painting in the living room.

Recalling the numbers from Jax Dunn's notebook, I retrieved it and began adjusting the dials according to the sequences noted. My instincts told me that these numbers were likely the combinations needed to unlock whatever lay behind the wall.

The prospect of discovering a hidden room filled me with hope. If Jax Dunn had safeguarded something of importance here, it might hold the key to saving Myles Henry and the others. With each turn of the dial, I felt closer to unraveling the mystery that had eluded me thus far.

After dialing in the twelve numbers, a section of the wall lifted, revealing a hidden secret room. It was about 200 square feet, carved from the original living room space. I stepped inside and switched on the light.

The room was filled with a haphazard collection of Egyptian antiques, including a striking gold mask typically reserved for the heads of pharaohs' mummies. Such an artifact was incredibly rare and valuable, hinting at the significance of the room's contents.

Making my way to the desk, I opened the first drawer and discovered a large stack of loose-leaf books bound together. The cover bore the title: "All Records of Unfortunate Experiences." It was Jax Dunn's diary.

Curiosity piqued, I began reading. Page after page drew me deeper into the narrative, until I lost track of time. The more I read, the more bewildered I became, as if transported back to a chaotic, ancient world.

Jax Dunn's diary, spanning five years, was a mix of succinct entries and elaborately detailed accounts. Some days were captured in two sentences, while others read like entire chapters of a novel, complete with dialogue and vivid descriptions.

Recognizing the importance of the diary's contents, I decided to present it unaltered, preserving its essence. The events chronicled were too bizarre and significant to be summarized simply.

Here begins Jax Dunn's diary:

July 6

The heat was oppressive today. An Arab approached me with twelve rubies, offering them at an astonishingly low price. Their beauty was breathtaking, undeniably genuine. The Arab was evasive, his manner mysterious, suggesting the rubies might have illicit origins, but he dodged all inquiries.

July 7

To ensure their authenticity, I sent the rubies to Paris for appraisal by the esteemed jewelry expert Balsamo. They were insured for a million pounds.

July 8

An urgent telegram arrived from Balsamo confirming the rubies as rare treasures.

July 9

I encountered the Arab again by chance while loitering outside a jewelry store. He approached me directly, asking, "Do you want to buy good gems, sir?"

"Yes," I replied, still cautious but intrigued.

"I have very good gems, sir. If you know the goods, you'll recognize I have real treasures, and I'm selling them at just one-thousandth of their market value. If you're interested, give me your address, and I'll send them to you."

Despite his dirty and unkempt appearance, something about the Arab's offer was compelling. This place was steeped in mystery, and perhaps, as with the rubies, something extraordinary might come of it. So I gave him my address, curious to see where this would lead. After all, the rubies he'd provided earlier had turned out to be genuine rarities.

Later, I returned to the street lined with jewelry stores and spotted the Arab once more. I approached him directly, noticing his wary, almost animalistic gaze. He spoke first, "Do you want some more gems?"

"Yes, I'm interested in top-quality green jade."

"Sir, all my goods are top-quality. Rest assured. Should I send them to the same address as before?"

"Yes, but I need them urgently. Can you deliver them in two hours?" My aim was to see whether he'd retrieve the gems immediately, allowing me to follow him.

He shook his head, "No, sir. Give me a day. I must travel far to get them. I'll deliver them to you by tomorrow morning."

His resolve was firm, and I had no choice but to nod in agreement.

As I turned and walked away, I reached the street corner, where I swiftly donned a mask, shed my coat, and slipped into the Arabic robe I had stashed nearby.

In mere moments, I transformed into an unremarkable Arab. Emerging from the corner, I noticed the Arab had vanished. I hurriedly pursued him, catching sight of his fleeting figure in a narrow alley. Step by step, I followed his trail.

I shadowed him closely, my mind racing with questions. How did he come by such exquisite gems? Was he linked to an international jewelry syndicate? Balsamo's telegram from Paris had stated that these rubies were unheard of—if traded publicly, there would surely be records. So, how had he acquired them?

I nearly lost track of the Arab several times, distracted by these thoughts. Eventually, about an hour later, he entered a shabby, low house, calling out, "Luda!" A response came, and he emerged with a short man. This man, no more than four feet tall, was even filthier than the Arab and had his head wrapped in a white cloth, revealing only his eyes. Such attire was typical for Arab women, but the man's gait and build suggested otherwise. His covered head only deepened my suspicions.

The pair continued walking, leaving the city behind and venturing into the wilderness. They seemed accustomed to long treks, and as darkness fell, it became easier to trail them unnoticed. Nearly ten miles later, we arrived at the ruins of a once-famous temple dedicated to the sun god—a place shrouded in history and mystery.

The temple loomed ahead, its silhouette stark against the night sky. I watched as they approached, wondering what secrets lay within and how it all connected to the enigmatic gems. This pursuit had led me here, and I felt on the brink of uncovering something monumental.

The temple, once a grand edifice, now lay in ruins with its massive stone pillars leaning precariously. It had long been abandoned, making entry difficult and dangerous. As I lay hidden in the bushes, just a few steps away from the Arab and the dwarf, I strained to listen to their conversation.

The Arab spoke softly, but his words were clear. "I hope you can identify the green jade," he said.

The dwarf replied in a voice that was unsettlingly dry and strange, "I can tell."

Despite the disguise, it was unmistakably a man's voice. They seemed to be retrieving the green jade, but from where? Had they brought the rubies here as well? Under the faint moonlight, all I could see were the gray-white stones and the remnants of the temple. There was no sign of any gems.

The dwarf lay on the ground, and the Arab covered him with his robe, concealing him completely. The dwarf then began to emit odd, indescribable sounds, his body quivering beneath the robe. This continued for a while before he fell still.

The Arab stood waiting patiently. The next hour dragged on tediously, but I was determined to uncover their secret, so I persisted.

Eventually, the dwarf stirred again, rising and wrapping himself in the robe. The Arab eagerly asked, "How is it? How is it?"

The dwarf's response was a simple, non-verbal "mmm."

I couldn't see his face, but I imagined it bore a troubled expression. They quickly retreated, leaving me to wonder what they'd been up to. Had they secured the green jade?

Continuing to shadow them, I followed them back into the city, returning to the grimy little house. It was nearly dawn. Having spent the entire night tracking them with no tangible results, I returned to my hotel, frustrated and exhausted.

July 10

After barely an hour of sleep, a knock at my door awakened me. The Arab slipped inside as soon as I opened it. My initial irritation dissolved when I saw what he placed on the table—six oval green jades. Each was priced at a mere thousand pounds. Even if they were fake, this was a steal given their apparent quality.

July 11

I spent the entire day pondering the origins of the green jade without any breakthrough, so I sent them off for expert evaluation.

July 12

Balsamo's urgent telegram arrived, incredulous: "Have you uncovered Solomon's treasure?" The jade was of exceptional quality, valued over 100,000 pounds each. Astounded, I knew I had to investigate further. I returned to the jewelry district, hoping to find the Arab, but he was nowhere to be seen.

Despite waiting a long time, there was no sign of him. Driven by curiosity and the potential for discovery, I retraced my steps to the squalid little house and knocked forcefully on the door.

"Who is it?" came the dry, strange voice of the dwarf, Luda.

Instead of answering, I shoved the door open. Inside, a short figure leapt up like a startled rabbit, attempting to flee but finding the exit blocked. He retreated into a corner, finally halting as he realized he was trapped.

Confronting Luda, a flood of questions raced through my mind. How were they acquiring such valuable gems? What was the secret behind the ruined temple and their mysterious activities? As I faced him, I knew I was on the brink of uncovering something extraordinary, something that could unravel the mysteries surrounding these enigmatic figures and their priceless treasures.

Without hesitation, I pushed the door open and entered the sparsely furnished room. The dwarf, startled, scrambled back into a corner, trying to escape but finding the exit blocked. In the dim light, I took in his unnerving appearance—his face was more lupine than human, with a protruding nose, bloodshot eyes, a crooked mouth, and sharp fangs. It was a visage that would certainly cause alarm if seen in public, explaining why he wore a hood outside.

After a tense five-minute standoff, he finally spoke in a halting voice, "You...what are you doing?"

"Are you Lu Da? Don't worry, I mean no harm," I replied, carefully choosing my words as his English was broken.

He nodded cautiously.

Pressing on, I said, "I also want some green jade. Green jade, do you understand?"

Another nod.

"I'll pay you—money, money!" I jingled two gold coins in my hand, watching as Lu Da's eyes widened with interest.

He took the coins eagerly, gripping them tightly. After a moment, he donned his hood, signaling he intended to fetch the jade. But as he reached the door, he suddenly tossed the coins back at me and bolted.

I stumbled back, bewildered, only to find myself confronted by a group of hostile Arabs. "Don't mess with Luda!" they warned menacingly.

I made a hasty retreat, shaken by the encounter. It had been an unsettling day.

July 13th

Friday the 13th—a day notorious for bad luck. True to form, the Arab was nowhere to be found, and Luda had vanished without a trace. Determined, I ventured to the abandoned temple, returning to the spot where Luda had been lying that night. The ground was marked by a large stone slab, akin to a foundation, with a small round hole just large enough for a fist.

Peering inside, I saw nothing, but when I pressed my ear to the opening, a hollow echo suggested a cavernous space below. Were the emeralds and rubies secreted away here? The prospect seemed too simple, yet irresistible.

I gingerly inserted my fist into the hole, stretching my arm as far as possible, but grasped only air. Panic set in as I struggled to withdraw my arm, fearing it might become lodged permanently — a predicament that would undoubtedly make headlines.

Grappling with both frustration and curiosity, I resolved to explore further. The hidden treasures of the temple and the enigmatic figures guarding them beckoned, promising revelations and dangers I could scarcely imagine.

July 14th

The previous day had been fraught with frustration, but I continued my search for the Arab. Unexpectedly, I discovered that Luda was also searching for him. However, when I approached Luda, he fled.

July 15th

The day yielded no results.

July 16th

Today turned out to be truly remarkable, a day filled with unexpected revelations. After waiting for two hours in the alley, I finally encountered the Arab again. I confronted him with a gun, hoping to intimidate him, and once we reached the wilderness, he divulged an astonishing secret.

The treasure was indeed in the small cave, but it lay in a cellar sixty feet underground. To reach the gems, one had to navigate through seven stone slabs, each about a foot thick. Each slab had a small hole, just big enough for a fist. Luda possessed the extraordinary ability to extend his hand sixty feet down to retrieve objects. As unbelievable as it sounded, the Arab appeared earnest.

Eventually, we located Luda and returned to the abandoned temple. This time, Luda inserted his arm into the small hole without the usual white robe. To my utter amazement, his arm detached from his shoulder and moved underground, sixty feet below. It was no illusion but a reality. What kind of power was this? What phenomenon allowed such a feat?

This power was far more alluring than any treasure. Luda, despite his magical ability, seemed simple-minded, and the Arab was not much brighter. It seemed that only the Arab knew this secret, but I believed it should belong solely to me, so I made the ruthless decision to kill the Arab.

Witnessing the Arab's death, Luda attempted to flee, but his left hand was caught. His hand detached from his wrist, and he continued to run, only to circle back, emitting strange, unintelligible sounds. Despite his struggles, his clothes tore, revealing a peculiar object hanging from a black hemp rope around his chest.

The object was difficult to describe, resembling a cigarette box, about two inches square. In the ensuing struggle to seize it, Luda managed to escape. Knowing I couldn't catch him, I resorted to using my gun. Luda was fast, but not faster than a bullet, and he was killed.

July 17

Having killed two people, I was plagued by strange hallucinations. Drinking seemed the only way to dispel them.

July 21

After four days of inebriation, I awoke in a hospital, still clutching the object I'd taken from Luda. No suspicion seemed to fall on me for the deaths of Luda and the Arab, and I quickly left the hospital for my residence. The object could be pried open, revealing two halves. One half contained thin metal sheets with numerous dot-like protrusions connected by fine lines, reminiscent of a miniature electronic board. Why did Luda possess such a thing?

The other half was composed of many thin sheets covered in strange symbols. What had been an extraordinary experience now became even more enigmatic. Despite the violence, I had acquired a wealth of gems at a bargain, securing some tangible reward.

July 22

Since departing, it felt as though the restless spirits of Luda and the Arab haunted me. The weight of their deaths lingered, entwined with the mysteries I had uncovered.

August 3rd

I remain clueless about the purpose or nature of the mysterious object. Despite consulting numerous experts, their reactions have been dismissive, often laughing at the strange symbols as if they were a figment of my imagination. It's frustrating and absurd.

September 7th

Today, I encountered Professor Gu Leqi, a specialist in ancient scripts. When I presented him with the text, he astonishingly declared it to be non-terrestrial in origin. As preposterous as this sounds, I couldn't shake the unease about the object that hung on my chest, albeit now with a platinum chain instead of the original black hemp rope. It's become a kind of keepsake.

January 1st

The new year arrived amidst celebrations, with ships in the harbor sounding their whistles. The object had been around my neck for half a year, so light that I barely noticed it anymore. But as the clock struck midnight, it emitted a peculiar sound.

It resembled the continuous "beeping" of a wireless telegraph. I left the festivities at once and retreated to a storage room to inspect it. As I opened it, the sound was clearer, and each tiny section began to emit a faint, mesmerizing flash.

The flashes were weak yet captivating, their strange colors both dazzling and unsettling. I had no idea of their origin or purpose.

This phenomenon persisted for ten minutes before ceasing.

January 2nd

I spent the entire day observing the object, but it remained inert, showing no signs of its previous activity.

January 3rd

Recalling my initial impression of the object's circuitry, I wondered if it might indeed be an advanced electronic device. I decided to consult an expert. My cousin Jimmy, an engineer at a large electronics firm in Canada, could offer insights. Perhaps he would uncover its secrets.

January 10th

Jimmy's assessment of the object was astonishing. He declared it a marvel of engineering, far beyond what Earth's technology could produce. He described it as a pinnacle of electronic design, with miniature electron tubes and circuits meticulously etched onto thin metal plates. Each of the seventy plates contained tens of thousands of electron tubes.

This meant the entire device housed at least seven hundred thousand electron tubes. It was an unparalleled computer, capable of feats unimaginable on Earth.

Given Jimmy's history of mental instability and a stint in a psychiatric hospital, his claims seemed dubious. Yet, his detailed analysis left me pondering whether his old tendencies had resurfaced.

(Such electronic boards are commonplace today. Decades ago, they existed only in the realm of imagination, highlighting the remarkable strides made in scientific progress.)

January 11th

Jimmy was relentless, constantly pestering me. I regretted involving him. He was adamant that his assessment was correct and insisted he could activate the "computer" on my chest using his factory's equipment. A "computer" with 700,000 electron tubes worn around one's neck—preposterous. I decided to distance myself from him.

January 12th

Jimmy returned, pleading once more. I reluctantly agreed and accompanied him to the factory. He attached the device to his chest, connected it with two slender wires, and powered it up. The wires linked to the factory's largest computer monitor, and suddenly, all indicators came to life.

Jimmy shouted with excitement, "Did you see it? Did you see it?"

As he yelled, factory guards and the manager rushed over, restraining him. In the chaos, I managed to retrieve the device and slip away, leaving Jimmy behind.

January 13th

After leaving Canada, I learned that Jimmy was committed to a mental hospital for damaging a multi-million-dollar computer. It seemed I was also wanted, but Jimmy wasn't entirely wrong. The device was indeed related to electron tubes. It was a computer, albeit not of earthly origin. This realization was bewildering. Was Jimmy truly insane, or was I losing my grip on reality? Who could say?

January 14th

Who was really losing their mind here?

January 15th

The device was indeed a computer, responsive to even the slightest electric current. Two dry batteries could make its protrusions emit a faint glow. But what was its purpose? I realized I needed to experiment further to understand. With no one to assist, I undertook these experiments alone, applying various currents and voltages.

January 16th

I was terrified—an experience unlike any I had ever faced. It was madness, sheer madness, beyond belief. I questioned my sanity. Should I admit myself to a mental hospital?

January 19th

After three days of drowning my fears in alcohol, I awoke with a calmer mind. Reflecting on January 16th, I realized it had all been real.

I could verify the reality of the event by repeating it, but I lacked the courage.

On that day, when the device encountered a 700-volt current, it emitted a bizarre flash. The colors were indescribable, encompassing every hue imaginable, yet it was fleeting. During the flash, my right hand vanished. My wrist was bare—no hand in sight. Where had it gone? I could feel it moving, but it was invisible, and my left hand couldn't touch it.

In a frenzy of fear, I bolted outside, and suddenly, I saw my hand gripping a bush. Trembling, I managed to reattach it to my wrist.

Was this insanity, or could my hand truly detach from my body? I recalled Lu Da and the gems. Lu Da seemed to possess a similar ability, but I dared not attempt it again.

This was utter madness!

December 20th

After a year of traveling the globe, I've returned and settled into a new home. It's on the 23rd floor of a serene building, offering a unique perspective on the world. During this year, I consulted many psychiatrists. They suggested that seeing one's limbs dismember or vanish could be a symptom of brain nerve splitting, potentially leading to madness if left unchecked.

Am I truly insane?

The device has been securely locked in a bank safe since I began my travels. I lacked the courage to confront it until now, choosing instead to avoid it.

But now that I'm back, the question of whether I suffer from brain nerve splitting has become pressing. Facing the device again requires immense courage.

Thankfully, I recall that the last unsettling incident occurred with a 700-volt current.

That night, after spending three hours contemplating the enigmatic device, I finally mustered the courage to activate the current with trembling hands.

The strange flash appeared once more. This time, because I leaned too far forward, the flash enveloped my head. Suddenly, it felt as if my entire body had lifted off.

However, it wasn't my whole body that flew up — something did, but it wasn't me.

To be precise, my head had detached and lifted.

Initially, I realized my body was missing. Then, I saw my body still seated on the chair, while my head had separated. After a moment of dizziness, my head reattached to my body.

There were no other changes. I was alive and felt no pain. The shocking part was witnessing my headless body sitting upright.

Although this was a perilous occurrence, experiencing it twice without harm made me bolder for a third experiment.

After regaining composure, I turned on the current again, directing the flash toward my right hand. My right hand disappeared.

Gingerly, I touched the spot with my left hand, confirming that my right hand was no longer at my wrist. It was truly absent.

It's astonishing to realize that even when my right hand is not physically attached to my wrist, it remains fully functional and under my control. The fact that my nervous system can command it despite the physical separation defies conventional understanding of biology and physics.

Searching for my detached hand was a bizarre experience, but eventually, I located it resting on the sofa.

I could still manipulate each finger, demonstrating that my nervous system could transcend physical space to control the hand. This discovery, though surprising, was undeniably real.

Fearing I might lose it, I quickly retrieved my hand and reattached it to my wrist. With each experiment, my confidence grew. After a brief rest, I attempted a fourth trial. Once again, my hand detached, but this time, I remained composed. I instructed it to open the window, and it did so effortlessly.

Curious about the range of this phenomenon, I commanded my hand to venture further. It flew out the window, scaled the wall, reached the platform above, and then returned to my wrist. This was a moment of unparalleled surprise and wonder.

The realization dawned on me: I wasn't losing my sanity. Instead, something extraordinary had happened, granting me abilities beyond imagination.

December 21

Continued experimentation revealed that I could detach and control not just my hand, but my feet and head as well. Each part moved independently, yet remained under my command. It's a marvel beyond anything I believed possible.

December 22

During one of my experiments, my detached feet were discovered by someone who, quite audaciously, kicked them. Although I couldn't see the person responsible, it demonstrated the vulnerability of my separated limbs. Despite these newfound abilities, I must remain cautious.

With the mysterious "computer" and its strange flash, I've transformed into something akin to a superhuman. This power is both exhilarating and daunting, opening a world of possibilities and challenges. Navigating this new existence will require wisdom and discretion, as I explore the limits and implications of my extraordinary abilities.

* * *

Jax Dunn's diary concludes its account of his own body parts here. What follows is a chronicle of his confrontation with the one who kicked him.

That person was none other than me, Ash Morris. The myriad disputes between Dunn and myself have already been meticulously detailed above, rendering further excerpts from his diary unnecessary.

The pages of Jax Dunn's diary unfurled a bewildering odyssey through phenomena that transcended rational comprehension. As I delved into his account within the shadowed confines of that clandestine room, I was engulfed by a maelstrom of disbelief and fascination.

Jax Dunn's writings suggest a reality where a mysterious device—something he refers to as a "computer"—emits flashes capable of separating limbs without pain, yet maintaining neural control. This notion is both fascinating and unsettling, challenging everything we know about the human body and physics.

While Jax Dunn would have no reason to fabricate such experiences in his private diary, the implications of his claims are staggering. What exactly is this device, and how does it function? The ability to detach limbs and still control them is beyond the scope of current scientific understanding.

These questions remain unanswered and continue to haunt my thoughts. The device's origins, its purpose, and the mechanisms behind its incredible effects are mysteries that demand further investigation.

Despite the disputes and history between Jax Dunn and me, this discovery is a testament to the mysterious and unexplored potential of technology and the human body. As I ponder these revelations, I am drawn to the possibility that there is much more to the world—and perhaps to ourselves—than we currently comprehend.

CHAPTER 12

The Origin of Abilities

The mysteries surrounding Jax Dunn and his discoveries continue to deepen. Why was he so determined to obtain the metal piece hidden within the mummy's sarcophagus? While Jax Dunn recognized some symbols on the piece, he indicated they were unrelated to modern languages or the phenomenon of limb separation. So what drove his obsession?

From Jax Dunn's diary and my own experiences, it's clear that at least three individuals have exhibited the ability to separate their limbs: the ancient Egyptian pharaoh, Lu Da, and Jax Dunn himself. For Lu Da and Jax Dunn, this ability stemmed from the strange device Jax Dunn termed a "computer."

But what about the pharaoh, whose limbs remained separated even in death? If this "computer" has existed on Earth for millennia, how could it have been activated in ancient Egypt, where high-voltage electricity was unknown and unused?

These questions swirled in my mind without resolution. I carefully placed Jax Dunn's diary in a brown paper bag, preparing to take it with me. As I turned to leave, I noticed something discarded on the ground near the table.

It was a small, thin object, about two inches square, gleaming with a curious metallic sheen. A gold chain attached to one side had been torn off.

The sight of it caused my muscles to tense involuntarily. Had I not read Jax Dunn's diary, I might have dismissed it as insignificant. But knowing its potential, I felt a mixture of fear and awe.

My heart raced as I instinctively stepped back. Yet, I reminded myself that the device's effects only manifested when powered. There was no need for fear at this moment.

I should have felt fortunate to have stumbled upon it. This device could potentially unravel the questions that haunted my thoughts. Steeling myself, I stepped forward, picked up the object, and examined it closely. It was indeed a metal box, surprisingly lightweight, with one smooth side and another dotted with needle-sized holes, two of which were larger and bore signs of electrical scorching—likely where power had been applied.

The box could be opened, its inner workings concealed within. To an untrained eye, it might resemble a lady's compact powder case. I opened it with little effort, revealing its contents.

Inside, as Jax Dunn noted, were extremely thin sheets, almost transparent and seemingly metallic. While Jax Dunn suggested they bore writing, I disagreed. To me, they resembled intricate traces, perhaps not words at all, but something else—something three-dimensional.

These traces hinted at a new form of science, possibly miniaturizing numerous devices onto a flat surface, yet maintaining their functionality. This thought occurred to me because the protrusions on the other half of the box resembled electronic circuit boards.

This discovery left me both exhilarated and apprehensive. Possessing such a device meant delving into the unknown, a realm where ancient mysteries and futuristic technologies converged. The journey ahead promised revelations, but also demanded caution and respect for powers that defied conventional understanding.

The realization that this small "powder box" could be both a massive computer and an electronic factory was staggering. Its complexity, hidden within such a compact form, was beyond anything I'd imagined.

As I examined the thin sheets, I noticed they were interconnected by incredibly fine filaments. In the secret room, I discovered a power generation device capable of producing high voltage electricity. The voltage meter confirmed that it could reach the necessary 700 volts.

Contemplating connecting the power supply, my hands trembled with anticipation and apprehension. Activating the device would reveal its function, but there was a significant risk. The strange flash could affect me, potentially detaching parts of my body, just as described by Jax Dunn.

The thought sent a shiver down my spine, and I instinctively placed the device back on the table. Suddenly, a safer plan occurred to me. I could connect the wires, step back, and then turn on the switch from a distance, allowing me to observe without being directly exposed to the flash.

Quickly, I inserted the wire plug into the two small holes on the device. After retreating six or seven steps, I activated the power.

Just as Jax Dunn described, the device emitted a flickering light. Curious to see the changes upon activation,

I had already spread out all the metal sheets on both sides of the box.

The two sheets, originally stacked, extended to about three or four feet when unfurled. As the strange flashes continued on the side with the raised points, a peculiar light suddenly emanated from a round black symbol on the other half.

This confirmed my earlier suspicion: the traces I had observed were indeed part of an instrument, carefully engineered and embedded within the sheets.

The light from this instrument was brief, lasting only about half a second. Had I been closer, I might have been caught in its beam.

After the light faded, the raised points on the other side continued to flicker. This reinforced my belief that the device functioned as an electronics factory. It seemed certain there was a method to control this "factory," yet the means to do so eluded me at present.

This discovery posed more questions than answers, but it also opened up a world of possibilities. Understanding and harnessing this technology could unlock secrets long buried in history, offering insights into both ancient and future technologies. The path forward would require careful study and experimentation, balancing curiosity with caution.

After about five minutes, when the flash reappeared, an inexplicable impulse surged within me. I yearned to hurl a part of myself into the light.

I had already lunged forward a few steps. Had my body not inadvertently brushed against the switch, plunging the room into darkness, I would have crossed that threshold.

With the switch off, the flash vanished, and so did my reckless impulse. Panting, I stood mere steps away from the anomaly, my heart pounding furiously.

At that moment, I realized that this artifact not only possessed an uncanny ability to sever human limbs but also wielded a profound influence over the mind. It emitted a kind of radio wave that seemed to perturb brain activity.

I lacked the courage to reconnect it to the power source, knowing its potential to warp human thought. The mere idea of confronting it again sent shivers down my spine. I hastily unplugged the wire, stowed away the delicate fragments, and sealed the box.

I then ascended the stairs, retrieved the metal piece along with Jax Dunn's translated inscriptions, and secured them before leaving the house.

Seeking refuge, I checked into a modest hotel, still grappling with the enigma of the metal piece and its connection to the artifact.

Initially, I attempted to decipher the cryptic words on the metal piece myself, leveraging Dunn's partial translation. Yet, despite my efforts, I was left with a garbled mess of incoherent words.

Had Myles Henry been here, he might have unraveled the entire text from these fragments. But now, Henry's mind was lost to us.

Jax Dunn's desperation for the metal piece was palpable. During our park encounter, he had already deciphered a fragment of the text, asserting that with just another 24 hours, he would be invincible and free of fear. This led me to surmise that the metal piece concealed a profound secret, likely containing crucial information — possibly the key to unlocking the enigmatic "box."

The translated text mentioned a high priest, described as the "incarnation of the bull god," with the power to revive the dead. His tomb, located underground ten miles east of the Zeus Temple, supposedly held the secret to his powers.

This piqued my interest; the tomb was possibly undiscovered, and unmarked on any map, promising the thrill of a groundbreaking find.

With a blend of trepidation and excitement, I prepared for the journey to uncover the high priest's tomb. The prospect of unveiling an undiscovered Egyptian tomb was tantalizing, transcending the mysteries of the device and the metal piece. It was a chance to step into history, to walk where few, if any, had walked before.

Before setting off, I visited Myles Henry in the hospital. Seeing him reduced to a childlike state, sucking his fist, was a poignant reminder of the stakes involved. I didn't walk in and try to talk to him, because just looking at his appearance was enough to make me feel sad.

I have also gone to the library to search for everything about the "Bertre Dynasty", but the historical records of this dynasty are not very detailed, and there is no mention of a great priest who transformed into a cow god. All of this is blank in history, and I will have to wait until I reach the tomb of the great priest to slowly excavate it.

According to the regulations, if a foreigner wants to excavate an ancient tomb, he must obtain the approval of the local government and be accompanied by a person designated by the local government. But I didn't apply for this because what I experienced would never be believed if I told anyone. If I applied, my application would definitely be rejected.

Two days later, I arrived at the main entrance of the great Zeus Temple. The Temple is indeed an extremely great building, and the clue I received was only "ten miles east". I could only use a compass to correct the direction, so I had to give up the normal travel route and move eastward in a straight line. Before going to the Zeus Temple, I rented a camel from a local who rented camels for tourists to ride.

The Arab, in halting English, inquired, "Sir, where you go? Need follow?"

I responded nonchalantly, "No, I'm heading east for quite a distance. I'll return the camel within three days."

The Arab sprang up as if he'd touched a branding iron. "Go east, long way?"

"Yes, what's wrong with that?" I asked, puzzled.

"You must be joking, sir. Your Arabic is excellent; how do you not know you can't go straight east

from here?"

I was taken aback. "Why not?"

The Arab scrutinized me for a moment before replying, "Three miles east lies the desert scorpion territory. This expanse spans over ten miles. Even the fiercest Kante Arabs wouldn't dare traverse it. You know, the desert scorpion!"

I was stunned.

Desert scorpions, I knew them well. Highly venomous, they blended seamlessly with the sand, nearly impossible to spot even with your nose inches away.

A sting from their poison-tipped tails would induce heart paralysis within seconds, leading to a swift, painless death.

The Arab's warning was clear: the path east was a death trap, infested with scorpions for over ten miles. What were my odds of survival if I ventured forward?

The sun dipped below the horizon, casting long shadows over the arid landscape as I stared, bewildered. "Even camels fear the venom of scorpions?" I whispered, my voice barely audible.

The Arab guide chuckled, mischief dancing in his eyes. "Everything fears these scorpions, my friend, even the might of Zeus himself!" he proclaimed, reaching for the reins of the camel he had rented to me. "Remember, you've only paid for three days' rent."

I protested quickly, "Surely, a fair price could make this camel mine?"

He hesitated, a dramatic sigh escaping his lips. "This camel, this noble creature, has been my companion for five years. A member of my family, sir. Parting with it would break my heart—"

Impatient, I slipped two crisp banknotes into his hand. "Twenty pounds. Done."

He stared at the money, silence stretching between us, before nodding fervently. "Yes, yes!"

In that moment, the camel was no longer family, but a transaction complete. I led it away, casting a glance back at the temple's entrance. The Arab was already huddled with others, pointing at me, his whispers carrying tales of a fool destined for the scorpions' lair to the east.

Fear gnawed at me, the desert scorpions a persistent threat. Few dared venture where I intended to go, where ancient sands concealed the tomb of a forgotten high priest. The allure of discovery surged within me; what secrets lay buried beneath the sands?

Determined, I altered my plan slightly. A camel's pace wouldn't suffice. I needed speed, protection — a car. I mounted the camel, urging it towards the bustling market near the Temple of Zeus, where I'd seen the vehicles of archaeological teams.

Under the cloak of dusk, I "borrowed" a small sports car, ideal for desert travel. Stealth was my ally; the archaeologists were lost in the hypnotic sway of belly dancers, oblivious to the world beyond their revelry.

I stocked up on essentials: disinfectants, a sharp surgical scalpel—precautions against the scorpions' sting. As I drove away, the market faded into the distance, a mere memory as the open desert stretched before me, daring me to uncover its hidden mysteries.

Returning to the Temple of Zeus, darkness had fully descended, and the crescent moon hung like a celestial beacon in the sky. Its silvery glow draped the temple in an ethereal light, casting shadows that danced atop the ancient stones and lending an air of mystery to the scene.

I parked before the temple, laying my compass beside me, and set my course due east through the nine majestic marble columns.

My only lead was a cryptic clue: "ten miles east of the temple." The vast expanse of desert stretched dauntingly ahead, and I couldn't help but question whether the high priest's tomb truly lay within those ten miles.

And even if I unearthed it, would I be able to decipher the enigma of the fabled "box"? The risks were monumental, almost enough to dissuade any rational mind from proceeding.

Yet, inexplicably, retreat never entered my thoughts. I pressed onward, accelerating into the night.

The car sped across the desert, its tires churning up waves of sand that billowed behind me in a golden cloud. But as I reached four or five miles, caution tempered my speed—I had entered the realm of the lethal scorpions.

Peering ahead, the moonlight painted the sand in serene hues, the dunes undulating softly in the gentle light. It seemed impossible that such tranquility could harbor mortal danger. For a moment, the temptation to abandon the vehicle and walk among the sands was strong.

But instinct held me back. I checked the odometer and compass, my pulse quickening as the car approached the nine-mile mark. Then, two monolithic cliffs emerged from the earth, their silhouettes rising ominously against the night sky.

The cliffs loomed tall and foreboding, framing a narrow canyon between them. As I approached, a sinking realization hit me—the chasm was a mere three feet wide. The car, my trusted vessel through the desert, was too broad to pass through.

I sat stunned, the path forward seemingly blocked by nature's ancient guardians. The night was silent around me, the moon casting its cool gaze as if daring me to find another way into the hidden depths beyond.

CHAPTER 13

The Grand Priest's Tomb

The canyon stretched before me, a narrow, shadowy alley winding about a mile into the distance. Somewhere at its mouth, perhaps, lay the tomb of the high priest, a treasure hidden by time.

Two choices confronted me: abandon the car and brave the canyon on foot, or attempt to circumnavigate the cliffs, a journey fraught with uncertainty. The rocky hills extended endlessly, their full breadth unknown, hinting that bypassing them might be an exercise in futility.

The decision was clear—I had to venture into the canyon.

With resolve, I slung a canvas bag over my shoulder and stepped into the canyon's embrace. Ten yards in, a shiver coursed through me as an ominous "click" echoed off the stony walls. It was my own teeth, chattering involuntarily, amplified into a spectral symphony by the sheer cliffs.

My heart skipped as I beheld the notorious desert scorpion. Before me was a grisly mound of bones, remnants of some unfortunate beast, now a playground for these venomous creatures. Their colors blended seamlessly with the rocks, rendering them nearly invisible—a trick of nature that sent a cold tremor down my spine.

Some scorpions lay still, others crawled, and a few locked in combat with their venomous tails. Their grotesque forms were unsettling, a nightmarish vision in the moonlit canyon.

Instinctively, I raised a foot to retreat, only to find the ground beneath me alive. What I thought were grains of sand began to stir — more scorpions, camouflaged so perfectly I had unwittingly trod upon them. The walls, too, teemed with these creatures, and the canyon became an impassable gauntlet.

I retreated swiftly, heart pounding, until I was safely ensconced back in the car. Only then did I breathe, relieved that no scorpions had hitched a ride on my person. The canyon would remain unexplored, at least for now.

Starting the engine, I drove onwards, navigating the rugged terrain in search of a passage. Thirty miles later, a potential route revealed itself, and I pressed on, the car bouncing over rocky hills until the first light of dawn. But with daylight came a new realization—I was lost amidst endless hills, low on fuel, a vessel stranded in a sea of sand.

The car's remaining gasoline would last a mere 15 miles, and yet, I was prepared for such an eventuality. Supplies for a week lay within reach, but the location of the high priest's tomb eluded me.

I climbed out, scanning the horizon. Sand and rocks stretched as far as the eye could see. I searched for the twin cliffs, landmarks that might guide me, but they were nowhere in sight.

My compass spun uselessly; without landmarks, it was a needle without direction. East held no promise of the tomb, and retreat was impossible. I was marooned, a lone figure in a vast desert expanse.

Exhaustion overtook me, and I retreated to the car, succumbing to sleep.

The sun had transformed the car into an unbearable furnace, jolting me awake with its relentless heat. Drenched in sweat, I stumbled out, gasping for air and gulping down precious water. The thought of the gasoline igniting under the midday sun weighed on my mind, a silent threat beneath the hood.

As dusk approached, the temperature finally relented, allowing me to resume my journey. I couldn't afford to linger indefinitely—I had to press on. The notion of a vulture circling above, waiting for me to falter, spurred me into action.

I drove cautiously, covering another five or six miles when a flicker of light caught my eye—a fire burning faintly ahead. Hope surged within me, and I steered the car towards the promise of human presence.

As I neared the fire, four Arabs in flowing white robes regarded me with wary eyes. I raised my hands in a gesture of peace, calling out in Arabic, "I've lost my way, may I approach?"

After a moment of silent exchange between them, one nodded. "Yes."

Lowering my hands, I approached the group. One of them inquired, "Where are you headed?"

Caught without an exact destination, I hesitated. Naming the tomb of the high priest seemed futile—they likely wouldn't know of it. Instead, I said, "I'm aiming for the exit of a canyon infamous for its scorpions."

Their expressions shifted to surprise. "You're heading to the exit of the Death Valley? Why would you venture there?" one asked, incredulous.

Thinking quickly, I concocted a plausible story. "I'm with the World Health Organization, tasked with researching desert scorpions. I need to reach the canyon's exit."

One Arab gestured southward. "Head south until you see two large stone pillars. That's your landmark."

I was puzzled. "Two large stone pillars? What does that mean?" I asked. The Arab responded matter-of-factly, "Two big stone pillars. That's two big stone pillars."

Pressing further, I said, "The exit to the east of the canyon is supposed to be a very remote place, but you said it's marked by two large stone pillars. What do you mean by that?"

The Arab replied, "Two large stone pillars. Everyone knows about them. Why do you doubt?"

A realization dawned. Perhaps these pillars marked more than a geographical feature—they could be the key to the high priest's tomb.

I expressed my gratitude and revved the engine, setting a course southward as instructed. With each mile, anticipation built within me. Could those stone pillars be the gateway to the secrets I sought? As the desert night enveloped me, the mystery beckoned, and I drove on, guided by the promise of discovery.

With less than ten miles to go, the car sputtered to a halt—the gasoline tank finally dry. The vehicle that had ferried me thus far was now a relic of the journey. I gathered my belongings and set out on foot, the desert stretching endlessly before me.

After some time, a towering black silhouette emerged against the night—a mountain, perhaps. Relief flooded through me as I recognized the familiar cliff face, a landmark that signaled I was near the canyon's mouth. But with relief came a twinge of dread; I was nearing the infamous scorpion nest.

The darkness enveloped the landscape as I switched on my powerful flashlight, its beam slicing through the gloom as I pressed forward. Two miles on, the light fell upon the two colossal stone pillars, standing sentinel in the desert night.

The sight of these monoliths took my breath away, revealing why the Arabs had been so incredulous at my doubt. By day, their grandeur would be visible for miles—massive structures, each rising thirty feet high, their circumference demanding the embrace of five men.

Crafted from enormous stones, each weighing no less than two tons, the pillars stood twenty feet apart, just yards from the canyon's exit. I approached, my steps deliberate, and examined the carvings etched into the stone surface.

Reliefs of bulls adorned the pillars, their forms both familiar and fantastical—some with bovine heads on human bodies, others purely animal, in all manner of strange configurations. The sight quickened my pulse. The bulls harkened back to the inscription I had translated: the high priest, an avatar of the bull god.

The presence of these bull motifs on the pillars confirmed my suspicions: the high priest's tomb lay nearby. Yet, I needed to find the entrance to this subterranean crypt. I scoured the ground with my flashlight, probing the sand with a sharp iron rod, searching for any sign of stone or hidden doorways.

An hour passed in exhaustive scrutiny, my body weary from the effort. I leaned against a pillar, resting, as the sky shifted from night to dawn. The first light of day crept over the horizon, prompting me to turn my back to the rising sun.

Suddenly, a revelation struck. The sun's ascent cast elongated shadows of the pillars onto the slanted cliff face. The two shadows converged, their tips meeting at a singular point on the rock. There, a narrow crack was visible, just wide enough for a person to slip through sideways.

The realization that I had stumbled upon the entrance to the high priest's tomb filled me with a surge of exhilaration. It seemed fortune had favored me, and I dashed forward, eager to unravel the secrets hidden within the ancient stone.

As I reached the base of the cliff, I marveled at my good luck. The morning sun had seemingly banished the scorpions, their presence nowhere to be seen on the rocks. Taking advantage of this, I began my ascent, adrenaline propelling me upward.

In just twenty minutes, I stood before the narrow stone crack. Given the grandeur suggested by the towering pillars, it seemed inconceivable that such a modest entrance could lead to the tomb of a high priest. Yet, upon closer inspection, it was clear that this fissure was a deliberate, albeit cleverly disguised, entryway.

The crack was the result of a large opening being skillfully sealed with stones of identical hue, leaving only a narrow passage. I switched on my flashlight, donned a gas mask, and cautiously ventured inside. A few steps in, I discovered a spiraling stone staircase descending into the earth.

The stairs, hewn from pristine white stone, were intricately carved, a testament to ancient craftsmanship. As

I descended, I monitored the air with test strips, which remained a reassuring light blue, indicating no presence of hazardous gases—a common peril in long-sealed tombs.

After more than forty steps, I reached a massive bronze door, its surface so polished it mirrored my reflection like a giant, ancient mirror. The clarity of the reflection drew me closer, curiosity piqued by how such an ancient door could maintain such a finish.

Then, the unthinkable happened. As I approached, the bronze door began to rise silently, smoothly, as though operated by some unseen mechanism. It defied the ages, an anachronism amidst the relics of time, leaving me awestruck.

Once the door was fully open, I stood at the threshold, my mind a whirlwind of disbelief and amazement. Peering through, I was met with a sight that defied all logic: a corridor illuminated by a series of lights, glowing softly from the walls.

These lights were not ancient oil lamps but something far more advanced. Each emitted a gentle, soothing glow, spaced evenly along the corridor, casting the space in a brightness akin to daylight.

I stood transfixed, the corridor stretching before me, its mysteries beckoning.

This was not merely a tomb; it was a marvel of engineering and foresight, a testament to a civilization that possessed knowledge beyond its time.

As I stepped forward, the air seemed to hum with the secrets of the ages, ready to reveal the wonders that lay beyond the bronze door.

I had come prepared for the dim and stifling atmosphere typical of ancient tombs, armed with all manner of precautionary gear and lighting equipment. Yet here I was, standing in a corridor brighter and fresher than any modern office — a stark contrast to the musty crypts of history.

I lingered at the threshold, shaking my head as though to dispel a dream. But no amount of shaking could alter the reality before me; the corridor remained, its air crisp and invigorating.

Compelled by curiosity and the impossibility of retreat, I ventured forward. The corridor's walls were smooth, and at its end, another door awaited. As I approached, it too swung open, seemingly of its own accord.

Beyond lay a hall, bathed in the same soft light. My hand shot to my hair, tugging at the roots in disbelief. This was no tomb filled with gilded relics; the furnishings were sleek, more akin to avant-garde Danish design than anything from antiquity. Their elegant lines defied immediate recognition.

How could this be possible? My mind reeled at the incongruity of the scene, a jarring juxtaposition of time periods.

I moved slowly, bewildered, toward a table that reflected my astonished visage — like a traveler from a bygone era confronted with the bewildering wonders of the future.

On the wall, two buttons beckoned: one red, one green. Nearby, two corresponding doors hinted at their purpose. This was no tomb—more like a place of futuristic elegance.

"Is there anyone here?" I called out, my voice echoing absurdly in the silence. The question itself felt ludicrous, as if I were intruding into a modern dwelling rather than an ancient priest's resting place.

But no response came, only the lingering reverberation of my voice in the vast hall.

The silence resumed, and I hesitated, hand hovering over the red button. My finger trembled, caught between skepticism and the unknown. What lay beyond that door? The question gnawed at me, my imagination spiraling with possibilities.

As I pressed the button, the red door swung open, revealing yet another room within the enigmatic tomb. At its center lay a long, transparent box. At first glance, it struck me as resembling a glass coffin. My heart skipped a beat as I peered closer, confirming my initial impression—it was indeed a glass coffin.

Inside, a figure lay at rest, their feet facing me. Draped in what appeared to be a white blanket, the figure's form was both familiar and profoundly alien. The head, larger than life, drew my focus first—wide at the top, tapering into a narrow base.

The sight was extraordinary. The head bore features that seemed more bovine than human: bulging eyes, short pointed ears, and two iron-gray, triangular protrusions jutting from the sides. It was as if I stood before a bull-headed man.

Yet, the hands and feet emerging from beneath the blanket were unmistakably human. The juxtaposition was startling—a fusion of human and bull, an embodiment of legends and myths.

The realization hit me with the force of revelation. This must be the high priest's tomb, the glass coffin housing none other than the high priest himself. The words from the metal tablet echoed in my mind: "The high priest is the incarnation of the bull god."

I lingered, rooted to the spot by a mix of awe and disbelief. How could such a being have existed? The notion seemed drawn from the realms of mythology and fantasy.

Slowly, I stepped back, lowering myself into a chair. My thoughts churned, grappling with the implications of what lay before me. The high priest—this bull-headed man—defied all earthly logic.

As I calmed, a hypothesis began to form, as implausible as it seemed. Could this high priest have been an extraterrestrial visitor, a being not of this world? The thought resounded with a strange clarity amidst the chaos of my thoughts.

The body in the coffin appeared perfectly preserved, untouched by the ravages of time. Its tomb was a marvel of engineering, and the being itself bore the hallmarks of a culture far beyond our own. This was no ordinary human.

The pieces started to fit together. The tomb's advanced construction, the priest's unique appearance, and the mysterious box — all pointed to something beyond the known history of Earth.

Rising from my seat, I felt a newfound sense of purpose. The discovery before me transcended the bounds of archaeology and history; it was a bridge to another realm of possibility. With renewed determination, I prepared to explore further, ready to uncover whatever secrets this extraordinary place had yet to reveal.

My gaze fell upon a peculiar device suspended above the glass coffin, reminiscent of a chandelier, though far more enigmatic. It consisted solely of two wires, each ending in a slender, silver-gray metal rod.

The sight of these rods ignited a spark of recognition within me. Instinctively, I reached for the mysterious "box" I had discovered earlier. The rods seemed to align perfectly with the larger small holes on one side of the box.

My hands trembled with anticipation and uncertainty. Could this device be connected to the box? The question loomed large in my mind, and the urge to connect the rods was overwhelming.

I battled with myself, urging restraint, cautioning against the unknown consequences of such an action. But like a moth drawn to flame, my resolve wavered. My hands moved almost of their own volition, defying the rational protests of my mind.

With an inevitability that felt almost predestined, I inserted the metal rods into the box's corresponding holes.

Once done, a strange sense of calm washed over me, as though the act had been necessary, inevitable.

I stepped back, heart pounding, eyes fixed on the box as it hung suspended, waiting for something to transpire. For a moment, all was still, the box remaining unchanged, its presence a silent enigma.

Gradually, a faint "squeaking" sound emerged, so subtle it barely surpassed the sound of breathing.

I stayed motionless, and soon, amidst the numerous tiny holes in the "box," two minuscule apertures began to emit streams of light. These holes, originally no larger than needle tips, produced light as fine as thread.

CHAPTER 14

The Two-Thousand-Year

Resurrection

The two beams of orange light, straight and laser-like, pierced the air with precision. I tracked their trajectory, and what I saw next left me astounded. The beams struck the forehead of the bull-headed priest within the glass coffin, creating a small ring of yellow light centered on his brow.

As I stood there, uncertainty clouding my thoughts, a sharp, piercing sound broke the silence. More beams of various colors erupted from the box, converging upon the coffin lid. And then, in a surreal moment, I witnessed the priest's hand twitch, as if stirred by an unseen force.

Instinctively, I lunged forward, yanking the box from its perch. The heat from the box was intense, forcing me to let it drop to the floor, its contents spilling out. I stepped back, heart racing, as I fixed my gaze on the coffin. The high priest lay motionless, but the image of his hand moving lingered in my mind.

Had my eyes deceived me? The thought gnawed at me, yet I couldn't dismiss what I'd seen. Could the beams of light have the power to resurrect the dead? The notion was preposterous, yet the high priest's apparent movement suggested otherwise.

The Bertre Dynasty, though distant in time, surely did not possess such advanced technology. But then, how could a man dead for over two millennia stir, even for a moment? The chill of the thought sent shivers down my spine, and I retreated from the room, breathless and shaken.

In the outer chamber, I gathered my thoughts, willing my racing mind to calm. I resolved to explore further, to uncover more of the tomb's secrets. Pressing the green button, I opened the corresponding door, revealing another stone chamber beyond.

This chamber was rectangular, its walls lined with instruments and glistening columns. A long table stood at its center, adorned with an array of small buttons. At the table's heart was a groove flanked by two metal plates, with a screen positioned before it.

The setup was astonishing, a testament to technology far ahead of its time. It surpassed not only the Bertre Dynasty but also the technological advancements of the 1960s. Yet, here it was, established millennia ago, a relic of the past yet a beacon of futuristic ingenuity.

What purpose did this chamber serve? What secrets did these devices hold? My mind raced with possibilities, each more incredible than the last. I was standing in a place where time and technology intertwined, where history and the future converged in a single, bewildering moment.

The chamber was indeed a marvel of technology, astonishingly advanced for something that had existed for three millennia. The buttons and switches, though adorned with text, were indecipherable — a language unknown, perhaps an ancient script or a code from a civilization far removed from any I knew.

With curiosity overriding caution, I pressed a few buttons at random, each action met with silence. The device remained inert, its secrets locked away. I continued my exploration, hands gliding over the table until they encountered a groove — an unmistakable match for the opened "box."

The groove was lined with needle-like protrusions, perfectly aligning with the holes on the side of the box.

Realizing this, I quickly returned to the previous room, retrieved the box, and placed it within the groove. The fit was seamless, as though the box was meant to be there.

As I unfolded the thin pages within the box, the metal plate exerted a magnetic pull, securing them in place. Instantly, the walls came to life with a constellation of lights, each dot illuminating in a pattern that seemed to pulse with energy.

A series of "beep beep" sounds filled the chamber, and a narrow slot produced a strip of paper, reminiscent of a telegram. It bore a series of black dots, an encoded message or language perhaps, but its meaning eluded me entirely.

While I puzzled over the dots, the TV screen flickered to life, casting a glow across the room. The image was chaotic, lines crisscrossing in disarray. I attempted to adjust the display by turning a few knobs, but the picture remained stubbornly unclear.

Then, a sound emerged from the device, faint yet distinct. It was not a language I recognized, but it was undeniably a voice—a message from the depths of time, a communication from the creators of this remarkable place.

The voice emanating from the screen was unmistakably human, yet its words were as foreign to me as the ancient sands of Egypt. My mind raced with the realization that this could be the language of a civilization long past, a language that had faded into oblivion with the passage of time. I was grappling with the impossible—understanding a tongue that no longer had speakers.

The frustration built within me as I listened to the unintelligible speech. The dots on the paper, the voice on the screen—they all held the key to unraveling the mysteries of this place, if only I could comprehend them.

Overwhelmed by the futility of the situation, I shouted in desperation.

To my surprise, the voice ceased as if acknowledging my cry. It was a clear sign that whoever—or whatever—was speaking could hear me.

I seized the opportunity, imploring for communication in a language I could grasp, hoping for a bridge across the chasm of time and understanding.

My pleas echoed through the chamber, but silence was my only answer. Then, after an eternity, the voice resumed, speaking in yet another unfamiliar language. Though I couldn't decipher it, the cadence and tone confirmed it was a language—a structured means of communication, even if I was not privy to its secrets.

A sigh escaped me, a manifestation of my frustration and helplessness, and astonishingly, a similar sigh followed.

It mirrored my own, conveying the same sense of exasperation. In that moment, I realized that the entity, like me, was unable to bridge the linguistic divide. We were both trapped in a dialogue of gestures and sounds, unable to truly connect.

I sank into the chair, resting my head on my hand, attempting to bring order to my chaotic thoughts. This situation demanded a new approach, one grounded in speculation and hypothesis.

The bull-headed figure in the glass coffin was likely not of this world, an interstellar traveler from a distant planet who had reached Earth in the ancient times of Egypt. His advanced knowledge and abilities could have easily led to his deification as the high priest, the living embodiment of a bull god to the people of that era.

The hypothesis that the voice emanated from the high priest's home planet made sense. The language was foreign, not of Earth, explaining my inability to comprehend it. If their understanding of Earth languages was limited to what the high priest had shared thousands of years ago, it was no wonder they couldn't grasp my modern speech.

The "box" seemed key to this entire mystery, perhaps an essential instrument for communication or power. Its loss could have triggered the strange occurrences I was experiencing. My theory felt plausible, but the question remained: how could I bridge the linguistic gap between us?

I sat there, contemplating, when the voice resumed, laden with urgency and frustration. It was as if the entity on the other side was pleading or reprimanding me, yet I felt equally helpless and exasperated, shouting back in futility.

Then, a thought struck me — what if the key to understanding lay with the high priest himself? I recalled the moment when the light beams had caused his hand to move. If those beams could indeed revive him, it might provide the only solution to this communication deadlock.

The notion of reanimating a being who had lain dormant for three millennia, possibly not even of Earthly origin, was both terrifying and intriguing. Yet, it seemed the only viable path forward. If the high priest could be revived, he might facilitate communication with his people, or at the very least, help me understand their language.

With the box in hand, my decision weighed heavily upon me. Removing it had silenced the voice and darkened the screen, confirming the box's integral role in this enigmatic setup. As I approached the glass coffin once more, I wrestled with doubt and curiosity. Should I attempt to revive the high priest?

The decision was monumental. On one hand, it could unlock the answers to the mysteries of this tomb and the civilization it represented. On the other, it might unleash unforeseen consequences. I stood beside the glass coffin, the weight of my decision pressing heavily upon me. The prospect of reviving the high priest was fraught with uncertainty, yet the desire to unravel the mysteries of this place drove me to action. With a deep breath, I connected the metal rods to the box, activating the beams of light once more.

As the beams pierced the air and struck the high priest, I retreated, anticipation mingling with trepidation. Minutes ticked by, each one stretching into eternity, until once again, I saw movement. The high priest's hand twitched, then lifted, confirming that I was not imagining things.

My heart raced, fear and curiosity intertwining as I considered the implications. What kind of being would emerge from this ancient slumber? A benevolent figure or a mindless entity, driven by instincts unknown? My mind buzzed with questions, each one more unsettling than the last.

With each passing moment, the high priest's movements grew more deliberate. His hands, elegant and dexterous, lifted the coffin lid as he slowly sat up. His transformation was mesmerizing, his eyes, which had been dull and lifeless, now shimmering with a spectrum of colors, like living kaleidoscopes.

As he turned his gaze upon me, those eyes settled into a deep, mesmerizing blue, evoking the depths of the ocean. It was clear he was fully conscious, fully alive.

With a fluid motion, he reached out and touched the box, extinguishing the lights with a practiced ease. The gesture was familiar, as if he were simply turning off a lamp, suggesting a deep familiarity with the device.

He fixed his gaze on me, his expression inscrutable, his bull-like face betraying no emotion. Yet, the eyes—those deep, shifting pools of blue—held an intelligence, a depth of awareness that was both reassuring and unsettling.

We stood there in silence, the air thick with unspoken questions and possibilities. This being, this high priest, held the key to understanding the enigma of his existence and the advanced civilization he represented. And as the silence stretched between us, I realized that this was the beginning of a dialogue that could redefine everything I knew about history, science, and the universe itself.

At that moment, he spoke. The sentence was simple, yet I couldn't comprehend it.

I was confronting a "person" who had been dead for three thousand years and resurrected—a being that was not of this Earth!

The shock and confusion I felt were overwhelming. I couldn't respond; I just stood there, paralyzed.

He stepped out of the glass coffin with deliberate slowness, advancing towards me. Desperately, I gestured for him to stop, knowing he wouldn't understand my words. I extended my hands, signaling him to halt.

To my relief, he paused. Thankfully, the gestures of our ancestors were not so different from our own.

After halting, he spoke again. I shook my head vigorously and spread my hands, indicating that I didn't understand.

His eyes changed color dramatically, perhaps reflecting his thoughts. He turned, retrieved a small box, ceased speaking to me, and walked into another room.

Hesitating briefly, I followed him. He adeptly placed the box on a groove in front of a control panel and began to operate it with remarkable skill.

Under his deft manipulation, lights flickered on the protrusions. Soon, the chaotic lines on the screen stabilized, revealing a very vague image.

Standing not far behind him, I could clearly see the blurry picture resembled a figure like the "high priest."

However, the image was so indistinct that I couldn't be certain it was a person.

Despite the blurry image on the screen, making it hard to discern if it was a person, I remained focused. Suddenly, the "high priest" began conversing with the voice I'd heard before, their exchange rapid and incomprehensible to me.

After thirty minutes, the "high priest" turned towards me, his eyes now a dark blue. He connected two thin metal wires to the center of his forehead, sparking with deep blue energy. I stood in shock, unable to fathom his actions. After three intense minutes, he shouted, "All right!"

To my surprise, his words were understandable. Recognizing my comprehension, he put down the wires and asked, "You understand what I said, right? You understand me?"

I quickly confirmed, "Yes, yes."

His relief was palpable. "That's great. I need your help. I hope you won't be as unfaithful as Pharaoh Beret."

While I understood his words, their meaning eluded me. What did "unfaithful as Pharaoh Beret" mean?

Confused, I replied, "Please forgive me, I don't understand."

Pointing to the TV screen, the high priest explained, "My companion informed me that I haven't contacted him for a long time—about three thousand years in your time. It seems he deceived me."

Still, I couldn't grasp the full picture and stared blankly at him.

Impatience colored his eyes anew. Waving his hand, he pleaded, "Can you help me? I want to go back. I've been delayed for too long."

An idea struck me. "Of course, I can help you, but I have conditions."

His eyes turned a fiery red as anger flared. "What conditions?"

Despite my fear, I stood firm. "I want to know everything."

The high priest advanced, forcing me to retreat until I was backed against a wall. "What... do you want?" I stammered.

"I want you to help me unconditionally!" he sneered.

For others, this might not be an issue, but my curiosity was insatiable. Not knowing the full story would be excruciating.

Though outmatched, I shouted, "No!"

He pressed down on my shoulders, incredulous. "No?"

"No. You must tell me who you are, where you're from, and what's happening. Detail everything, and I will help you."

The high priest's eyes grew redder, resembling twin furnaces. We stood at an impasse for two minutes before he spoke again, "First, I want to ask you: who are you, what is the current state of Earth, and how did you get here?"

CHAPTER 15

Earthlings as Ants

The question hung in the air like an unsolvable riddle. How could I possibly convey the vast and incomprehensible changes Earth had undergone over the last three thousand years to someone who had been absent for so long? The world he once knew was now an enigma even to its current inhabitants.

Faced with the high priest's inquiry, I could only shake my head. His eyes softened, yet his words were sharp, cutting through the silence with cold precision. "Earthlings," he declared, "are the embodiment of meanness, cowardice, and shamelessness. Are you truly any better than Pharaoh Beret?"

His fixation on comparing me to an ancient Egyptian pharaoh was baffling. Had he been deceived by that long-gone ruler? But what power could a pharaoh have wielded that could outmatch the high priest's formidable abilities? The mystery deepened with his bitter resentment, echoing across the centuries.

"I don't understand," I admitted, striving for clarity amidst the confusion. "The Pharaoh you speak of—I have no knowledge of his dealings with you."

The high priest slumped into a chair, his great, bull-like head cradled in his hands. He punched buttons on the control panel with a certain urgency, conversing with his companion in a language that eluded my understanding. Their anxious tones betrayed the gravity of their discussion.

Eventually, he returned, grasping my shoulder with an intensity that sent a shiver down my spine. "I possess the scientific means to analyze every substance on Earth," he declared, "yet I cannot decipher the truth of human nature. Are you honest or cunning?"

I drew a deep breath, aware that he knew little of human intricacies. "Understanding a person is no simple task. Even the most deceitful can be moved by sincerity. Treat them with honesty, and they might hesitate to betray you repeatedly."

"Rubbish," he retorted, his voice laced with frustration. "Do you think I am naive? I refuse to be deceived again."

I regarded him steadily, a calm settling over me. Despite his exceptional capabilities, it was clear he needed my help. And if he sought my assistance, why should I fear him?

"Honesty must be mutual," I proposed. "If you desire truthfulness, then be truthful yourself. Tell me your story, and perhaps we can find common ground."

His eyes flared with anger, a fiery red that threatened to consume. "I could erase you from existence!" he roared. "Your Earthly laws of matter's indestructibility are laughable to me."

Yet my resolve was unshaken. "I believe you possess such power. Perhaps you could annihilate everyone on Earth, but your real challenge lies in the need for an Earthling's aid, correct?"

His eyes, ablaze with fury, seemed to burn with an intensity that could ignite the world. Yet behind that rage, I sensed desperation — a need for resolution, for understanding, and perhaps, for redemption.

His laughter echoed through the chamber, a sound laced with both condescension and intrigue. "I can satisfy your curiosity," he declared. "I hail from a celestial body far from Earth."

"I suspected as much," I replied, acknowledging the advanced nature of his civilization, which had far surpassed our own.

"The High Priest" nodded, his admission swift and unapologetic. "Indeed, the position of earthlings in our hearts is akin to that of ants and bees in yours."

His words stung, a dismissal of our entire species as mere insects. Anger simmered beneath my skin, but I held my tongue, eager to hear more of his story.

He sensed my discontent, a sneer curling his lips. "Consider this box," he continued, gesturing to the enigmatic object. "It is a miniaturized electronic factory, capable of wonders beyond your wildest dreams. Perhaps you've envisioned such a marvel, but in your minds, it would span a city. Yet here it is, compact enough to carry."

I remained silent, feeling the weight of his technological superiority. In that moment, I did feel like an ant beneath his gaze.

His finger lingered on the box. "If harnessed for power, it could provide endless electricity, enough to sustain your planet for eons."

I interjected, attempting to curb his arrogance. "I understand. But tell me more about yourself."

He paused, his gaze narrowing. "Our kind intended to migrate to Earth, to establish a new home. But fate intervened."

"What happened?" I asked, intrigued by the tale unfolding.

"Two asteroids collided, unleashing a chain reaction. A radiation ring formed, impassable by our ships. I alone reached Earth."

The enormity of his words sank in, my palms damp with sweat. The randomness of cosmic events had altered the course of history, sparing humanity from a fate of subjugation or extinction.

"Without that collision," he continued, "your people might have become our subjects long ago, reduced to the status of mere insects."

The thought was chilling, a stark reminder of our insignificance in the grand scheme of the universe. Yet here we were, shaped by chance and cosmic whimsy.

"I was stranded," he said, "but communication endured. I remained on Earth, ascending to the role of high priest during the Beret Dynasty. My skills were undeniable."

"The ignorance of Earthlings is unfathomable," the high priest intoned, his voice dripping with disdain. "Yet, I managed to compel them to construct these three stone chambers. All the while, I maintained communication with my celestial brethren, waiting for the radiation ring to dissipate or for us to find a means to destroy it. But thus far, we've failed."

"Waiting for three thousand years?" I interjected, incredulous.

He laughed, a sound that echoed with contempt. "The absurdity of your concept of time is yet another testament to your species' ignorance."

His derision was relentless, and though he ridiculed Earthlings with impunity, I found his critique of time itself baffling. Time was as intrinsic to us as breathing. "What's so amusing about time?" I challenged.

"Consider this," he replied, eyes gleaming with a knowing glint. "What would you do if you had only three months left to live?"

His question caught me off guard, but there was only one honest answer. "I'd be terrified," I admitted.

"And if you had only three days?" he pressed.

"Even more so," I confessed, unease twisting in my gut.

"Exactly!" he exclaimed with a triumphant laugh. "The closer one is to death, the greater the fear, anxiety, and despair. Yet, every Earthling knows death is inevitable, their ultimate end. Still, they are ensnared by time, frantically pursuing power, wealth, engaging in conflict, and committing atrocities. Isn't that laughable?"

"Then what about you?" I retorted. "Are you immune to death?"

His laughter continued, a strange, hollow sound. He offered no answer, and I sensed his mockery hid a deeper truth—that he was not so different from those he ridiculed.

Eventually, his laughter subsided. Unwilling to delve further into such an existential debate, I steered the conversation back. "You were telling me about your situation. Please, continue."

He released my shoulders, shaking his head. "Continue? Very well. We've waited long, and despite our scientists' best efforts, the radiation ring remains impervious. But recently, they devised a way for me to return."

The revelation struck me like a bolt of lightning. If the high priest could return to his celestial home using this technology, what was to stop an entire invasion from his kind? The implications were staggering, a potential threat to Earth on an unimaginable scale.

As I grappled with the enormity of this possibility, the high priest continued, his voice a mix of pride and determination. "It's a risky method," he explained, "but by reorganizing components of the computer, I can emit a light capable of decomposing the body's original structure — down to trillions of atoms."

My mind raced, struggling to comprehend. "So, you're essentially vanishing," I blurted out, the concept both fascinating and terrifying.

"Indeed, a temporary vanishing," he confirmed, his tone almost serene. "The atoms of my body, propelled by the decomposition light, travel at the speed of light. Once they reach my home planet, they reassemble, forming my body anew, bypassing the radiation belt."

His words painted a picture of science so advanced it bordered on the miraculous. I was silent, absorbing the magnitude of what he described.

"I've tested the computer, refined its capabilities," he continued. "That light can reduce any living being to its elemental form—"

A thought struck me, interrupting his narrative. "This decomposition light—what happens if it only touches a hand?"

"The hand would disappear," he answered matter-of-factly.

"Forever?" I pressed, my mind tracing the implications.

"Not at all. The atoms persist, free in space, waiting to reform."

"That's not what I mean," I interjected, the pieces falling into place. "This light has turned Earthlings into fragmented beings, their limbs capable of detachment."

The high priest nodded, unfazed. "When the computer's power supply is insufficient, such anomalies occur. The light decomposes but lacks the power to transport the atoms, causing them to return to their original state. The nervous system remains inexplicably connected, allowing a hand to function independently until proximity draws it back."

His explanation resonated with what I knew of Jax Dunn's plight—a man believing he wielded a miraculous power, unaware it was a mere side effect of insufficient energy.

I nodded, my understanding deepening. "So why haven't you returned to your world?"

The high priest's eyes flared an angry red, his frustration palpable. "I was ready," he growled. "I sought King Bertre's aid, trusting in our friendship. Though confused by my residence, I believed he'd assist me. "

This is fairly straightforward to grasp. As a modern individual, I was bewildered upon arriving here. Imagine the confusion for someone from three thousand years ago encountering all this!

"I first anesthetized myself and lay inside. I instructed him to press the buttons. Once powered on, the decomposition light would break me down and transmit me at the speed of light. Yet, he failed to do so!

"Perhaps he pressed just one button, and the resulting function from the computer had a profound inhibitory effect on my entire bodily tissues and nerves, placing me in prolonged hibernation. He removed the computer, leaving me in stasis until you arrived!"

I began to grasp why the Grand Priest cursed humanity with such contempt and why he was initially so hostile towards me. He had been deceived.

Originally, he could have returned, but instead, he "hibernated" for nearly three thousand years!

Why the Pharaoh suddenly changed his mind remained a mystery. I speculated that the "box" must have fallen into the Pharaoh's hands. Three thousand years ago, people couldn't have fathomed what that "box" was.

Perhaps the Pharaoh used it as an ornament and passed it on. Maybe lightning or some other event triggered the "box" to activate, shattering the Pharaoh's body—the strange mummy discovered by Professor Henry!

After that, the box might have been deemed an "ominous object" and abandoned until modern times, eventually falling into the hands of an Arab dwarf before being passed to Dr. Henry.

Of course, this was all speculation, as everyone associated with the 'box' had long since perished.

While I was lost in thought, the Grand Priest looked at me and said, "Now, I need your help too. You must help me."

My mind was in turmoil. I stammered, "Of course, it's possible. Since I woke you from hibernation, I'm also willing to help you."

"That was just a coincidence, wasn't it?" The Grand Priest's words were cunning. Although I had revived him by chance, couldn't he at least thank me for it?

I chose not to argue. "At least it shows I mean you no harm."

Satisfied, the high priest beckoned me to follow.

The high priest said, "That's good. Come with me, and I'll show you which buttons to press. You must press all seventeen buttons continuously. If you only press one and stop, I will enter hibernation again! And once I am in hibernation, using this 'box' will wake me up, just like before. Now, observe carefully!"

As he spoke, he operated the control panel. Although I grasped it after two tries, he insisted on teaching me twice more, ensuring I could perform the sequence without error.

Then, I saw him take a metal bottle and put it in his mouth. With a "hiss," something sprayed into his mouth. He discarded the bottle and said, ""Use this method to send me back, and if it proves effective, I believe it won't be long before our returning to Earth. At that point, you'll be the most powerful person on Earth."

His words sent my heart racing and my expression shifting drastically. The thought that suddenly sprang to mind was one I had to conceal. I quickly turned away. "I know. Are you still sleeping in that glass box? Let me handle it!"

The high priest nodded and lay down in the glass box. I watched as the light in his eyes faded. Finally, he lay still.

I knew he had fainted, but my heart pounded even harder. I couldn't tell if I felt elated or remorseful; it was a complex mix of emotions.

In the midst of my chaotic thoughts, a sentence the high priest had spoken rang clearly in my ears: "I can analyze everything and understand the composition of everything, but I cannot understand people."

No matter what planet he came from or how advanced his scientific knowledge was, he could never truly understand human thoughts.

Not only is it impossible for one person to fully comprehend another, but even understanding oneself is a daunting task!

For instance, ten minutes ago, I was determined to help the high priest, but his last words changed my mind.

This was a sudden decision. Not only did the high priest not foresee it, even I hadn't anticipated it moments before changing my mind.

After I saw the "high priest" lying down, I slowly approached the control panel.

My fingers trembled slightly as I pressed the first button forcefully. The "box" suspended in the air emitted a "squeaking" sound that persisted for about three minutes before ceasing.

This was when I should have pressed the second button.

Instead, I stepped back and approached the glass coffin, glancing at the "high priest." He lay there, just as I had found him.

I removed the "box."

Doing so would place the "high priest" back into a "hibernation state."

Yes, that was my intention, and this was my new resolution.

I had originally planned to help him return to his celestial body via "atomic decomposition," but upon hearing that they could soon arrive in large numbers after his return, I reconsidered.

Despite his promise that I would become the most powerful man on Earth, this so-called "most powerful man" would actually be a puppet under the rule of beings like him!

CHAPTER 16

Unexpected Rescue

In the tangled web of my thoughts, a single decision crystallized with the clarity of a laser beam: I preferred the precarious freedom of an ordinary civilian to the gilded chains of being the "most powerful" puppet. This epiphany propelled me to act.

I opened the enigmatic box, its thin metallic sheets glimmering ominously, and attempted to tear them apart. My efforts were futile, my hands rendered clumsy by the tremors of fear that rippled through them. The specter of the Great Priest awakening loomed large in my mind. Should he discover yet another betrayal, the repercussions would ripple far beyond me, engulfing countless innocents in their wake.

Realizing the futility of destroying the box with my bare hands, I folded it away with care, concealing it within my bag. Resolute, I seized a stone stool and brought it crashing down upon the control panel with all the force I could muster. The neighboring room's scientific apparatus met the same fate, my frenzied assault plunging the "grave" into an abyss of darkness.

I navigated the pitch-black labyrinth by memory, retreating through the corridors until I emerged from the mountain's crevice into the open air.

As I crawled free, dusk embraced the landscape, the setting sun casting a blood-red hue over the flat expanse of sand. Despite the desolation, a profound warmth suffused my vision—I had returned to the realm of humanity.

Moments earlier, entombed within the Great Priest's domain, I had felt severed from the world of men. Now, liberated, I descended the mountain, retrieving explosives from my bag. Initially, these were my contingency for breaching an ancient tomb—a tomb that, I had discovered, was far from ancient, a relic from a future that defied my understanding.

But now, these explosives served a different purpose. Scaling the mountain once more, I wedged them into the rock's crevices, set the fuse, and ignited it. Then I sprinted away, the earth beneath my feet trembling with impending destruction.

A thunderous roar shattered the evening calm. I flung myself to the ground as a storm of sand engulfed me, a gritty deluge that buried me in its wake. I clawed my way to the surface, emerging to survey the aftermath.

The explosion had effectively sealed the mountain's crevice, consigning the secrets within to eternal obscurity. No one would ever know that buried beneath the rubble lay three enigmatic stone chambers, nor that within them slumbered a bull-headed figure, a relic of an ancient Egyptian dynasty, hailing from a distant celestial body. His hibernation, once spanning three millennia, would now likely endure far longer, perhaps indefinitely. And even if he were discovered, the mechanism to awaken him—the box—would be gone, obliterated by my hand.

As the echoes of the blast faded into silence, I emerged from the sand, the gritty residue of my escape clinging to my skin. Standing upright, I was met with an unsettling sight: a legion of poisonous scorpions, thousands strong, poured from the canyon like a living flood, their movement a sinister whisper against the earth.

My heart seized in my chest as I turned and ran, the urgency of survival propelling my legs faster than the scorpions' multitude of skittering appendages.

With each stride, I shed my burdens — gear and provisions cast aside in desperation—until only a solitary water canteen remained. Mercifully, my car appeared on the horizon, an oasis of safety in the barren expanse. It was only upon reaching it that I dared to glance back, my pulse quickening as I saw the tide of scorpions, a mere twenty steps behind, their advance relentless and terrifying.

The sight was primal, a visceral nightmare come to life. I lunged into the car, slamming the door shut as the engine roared to life. Yet dread clutched at me anew—the fuel gauge languished at empty.

I was utterly drained, my legs refusing to carry me further. With no other choice, I sealed myself inside the car, winding up the windows and locking the doors with trembling hands.

The scorpions surged like a living tide, swarming over every surface. They clambered over the roof and cascaded down the windows, their sinister forms outlined against the fading light. Their venomous stingers tapped against the glass, a chilling reminder of the deadly threat they posed. I shrank back, feeling the walls of my sanctuary close in as the air grew stale and my breaths became labored.

Opening the window even a crack was unthinkable, despite the mounting pressure in my chest. I endured the suffocating claustrophobia, clinging to the hope that this nightmare would pass. The scorpions, it seemed, were intent on moving forward, not lingering. But how long would it take for such a vast horde to disperse?

Thankfully, it was night. The cooler air meant I could hold out longer in the sealed car. Eventually, the relentless swarm subsided, and I dared to crack open the window, drawing in the fresh air with desperate gratitude. Yet caution held me captive; I remained inside until the first light of dawn assured me the danger had passed.

Emerging into the dawn light, I realized the daunting task ahead. Without the car, my journey back would have to be on foot—a grueling trek across the desert's expanse. Each step was a struggle, the sand shifting treacherously beneath my feet.

Despite losing nearly everything, I clung to the pot of water. It was my lifeline, a precious resource that I rationed carefully. I calculated that it would sustain me for two days, just long enough to reach the Temple of Zeus. But the specter of the scorpions haunted my thoughts; encountering them again would spell certain doom.

Fortune, however, smiled upon me. After over thirty hours of relentless walking, exhaustion threatened to overwhelm me. When I finally collapsed, it was not onto the desert sand, but upon the stone steps of the Temple of Zeus.

In that moment, relief washed over me. I had made it— surviving not just the elements, but the harrowing ordeal of a discovery best left buried. The secrets of the past were safely sealed away, and I was free to breathe the air of the present, grateful for the chance to continue my journey.

The scene was a whirlwind of activity, a cacophony of voices swirling around me as curious onlookers gathered. I ignored them, focusing only on the moment I was lifted by a policeman and whisked away to the hospital.

My recovery was swift, but the police visit was unexpected. Their demeanor was brusque, urging me to leave town with a distinct lack of warmth. Unsurprisingly, I chose to keep my harrowing adventure to myself.

Discharged and ready to depart, one task remained: a visit to Myles Henry. His situation weighed on me, demanding resolution. It took multiple attempts before I gained access to him at another facility specializing in neurological disorders. Yet, even then, I was shadowed by two individuals claiming to be from the "hospital," though their true affiliation with law enforcement was evident.

The hospital's heightened security was perplexing. Henry, now a mere shell of his former self, posed no threat. Why, then, did the police—or rather, the hospital staff who were clearly officers in plainclothes — maintain such vigilance?

Accompanied by my escorts, we navigated a labyrinthine corridor to the heart of the circular building, an open space dominated by a solitary, forlorn structure. Guards patrolled its perimeter, heightening my suspicion. "What's going on with Dr. Henry?" I inquired, my unease growing.

"Nothing new," came the curt reply.

"Then why all the security?" I pressed.

Their response was dismissive, "We know our duties."

The aloofness of these men was infuriating, but I held my tongue, noting the ostensibly hospital-attired personnel outside the house were unmistakably police. As I approached the door, my path was blocked. "Sir, you can't enter," one of them declared.

Outraged, I protested, "But I'm here to see Professor Henry!"

"You're allowed to see him," they insisted, "but only through the window. His room is below."

Their emphasis on "see" was grating, a bureaucratic loophole meant to placate without fulfilling. Frustrated, I retorted, "I intended to visit him, not merely glimpse him through glass."

They shrugged, hands raised in helplessness. "We're just following orders."

I clenched my fists, anger simmering, but the presence of nearly a dozen guards deterred any rash actions. A confrontation would only ensure I never saw Henry.

Resigned, I acquiesced, "Fine, lead the way."

We moved a short distance to a window, where they gestured, "He's inside."

Peering through the glass, I had to press my face close, the glare obscuring my view. What I saw sent a jolt through my body. I stumbled back, gasping for breath.

In the dimly lit room, a face emerged from the shadows—bloated, pallid, and fixed with a vacant grin. The visage was alarmingly close, separated from mine by mere centimeters of glass.

The face in the window was a grotesque parody of the Henry I once knew. The proximity was unnerving, the glass a fragile barrier between us. As I recoiled, trying to regain my composure, the face remained fixed in its eerie grin, a haunting mockery of its former self.

Turning to my escorts, I asked, "Is this really Dr. Henry?"

Their nods confirmed the grim reality. The transformation was incomprehensible, a stark contrast to the vibrant, intelligent scholar I had expected to see. The encounter left a chill that lingered as I exited the hospital, my mind struggling to process the change.

Outside, I paused, trying to steady my racing thoughts. The two officers shadowed me, their presence a silent reminder of the gravity of the situation. One spoke, his tone edged with barely restrained frustration, "Because of you, sir, six of our finest have ended up like this. We advise you to leave quickly, before we lose our restraint."

His words struck me like a blow. The notion that I was somehow to blame was absurd, yet their grief was palpable, their patience wearing thin. The implication was clear: my continued presence was a provocation they could no longer tolerate.

"I could argue my innocence," I replied, "but it's clear that's not the solution here. I'm leaving for the airport now."

I flagged down a taxi, urgency propelling me into the back seat. "Airport," I instructed, as the vehicle accelerated away.

The car sped forward, my mind a whirlwind of confusion. I couldn't even muster the courage to glance out the window, fearing that Henry's ghastly, idiot visage might suddenly materialize outside. As this thought gripped me, I froze, and an involuntary shout escaped my lips, "Stop!"

The streetcar driver pulled over, casting a wary glance in my direction. The urgency of my thoughts consumed me, a critical realization just within reach. I needed clarity, uninterrupted by questions or distractions. "Keep driving," I insisted, "but slower. No questions, just follow my lead."

His expression was a mix of shock and suspicion, likely pegging me as another eccentric escapee from the renowned brain hospital. In a way, this worked to my advantage; the less he interfered, the better.

As the car crept forward at a leisurely pace, my mind pieced together the fragments of my revelation. The fear of seeing Henry's face outside the window had triggered a deeper inquiry. Under what circumstances could his face appear like that? The answer was unsettling: if Henry were a fragmented person.

The implications of this were staggering. If Henry's head could detach and move independently, it might suddenly appear anywhere, even at my car window. But what did it mean if Henry was indeed fragmented?

The high priest's words echoed in my mind. Jax Dunn's disembodied hand wasn't merely severed; it underwent a rapid, complex transformation. The decomposition light broke it down into atoms within a fraction of a second. Invisible to the naked eye, these atoms reassembled at a distance, maintaining their original configuration. Crucially, the nervous system's electric impulses continued to command the limb from afar.

If Henry's head had undergone a similar process, what were the implications for his condition?

The high priest mentioned that the atomic reassembly adhered strictly to the "original situation." This phrase now held profound significance. If Henry's brain, ravaged by drugs, were to disintegrate and reform, would the "original situation" mean a return to his pre-damaged state?

If the restoration meant reverting to the state before drug-induced damage, Henry could be healed entirely. Even if not, there was nothing to lose.

I recalled the numerous encounters with Jax Dunn. His injuries always healed with improbable speed. Was this due to the decomposition and reassembly process resetting to the "pre-injury" state?

The realization was electrifying. I shouted, "Stop, stop!"

The driver complied, stopping at the airport entrance. "Sir, isn't this your stop?" he asked, puzzled.

"No, I've changed my mind," I replied, shaking my head.

His reaction was swift and dramatic; he leapt from the vehicle and bolted as if fleeing a madman. I watched him go, understanding his fear but having no time for reassurances.

I slid into the driver's seat, turned the car around, and sped toward the police station. Upon arrival, I burst through the doors, intent on sharing my revelation. Yet, the atmosphere inside was tense, the officers eyeing me with a mix of curiosity and apprehension.

I forced a smile, trying to convey calm amidst the palpable tension. "Please, allow me to see—" I began, but before I could finish, two officers advanced, their demeanor menacing.

"Get out!" one barked, cutting me off. "Go back, leave our country!" Their hostility left no room for negotiation, and I retreated, step by step, until I was out the door, a third officer leveling his gun as a stark warning.

I slammed into the driver's seat of the streetcar, adrenaline propelling me away from the station. The officers' vehement reaction was unexpected, a stark contrast to the urgency of my mission. I had come to them with a glimmer of hope—a theory that Myles Henry's condition could be reversed through atomic decomposition and recombination. The box, still in my possession, held the key. A 700-volt current could activate the decomposition light, potentially restoring Myles Henry.

But they hadn't listened.

With resolution hardening into determination, I realized I'd have to rescue Henry myself. The thought of infiltrating the ward was daunting. I'd never attempted something so audacious—liberating a living person from confinement.

Contemplating the logistics, I made a pit stop at a local hotel, allowing myself a day to strategize. Jax Dunn's residence offered a clandestine refuge, a place to execute my plan without interference.

The following night, under the cloak of darkness, I infiltrated the hospital. Security had slackened since my last visit, and extracting Henry proved less formidable than anticipated. Disguised in white uniforms I had procured,

Henry and I slipped out, blending into the night and making our way to Dunn's abode.

Once there, I seated Henry and connected the box to a power source. My heart pounded as the decomposition light struck his head. The process unfolded in an infinitesimal moment, atoms scattering and reassembling with precision.

Henry's astonished voice rang out, "Oh my God, where is my body?"

From my vantage point, his head had vanished, momentarily detached. Yet, to Henry, now cognizant and whole, it was his body that had disappeared, leaving his head three steps away. I swiftly cut the power, and in an instant, his body rejoined his head.

Success!

I used the same process to restore the other experts. When Dr. Henry reappeared at the police station, whole and coherent, the officers' attitudes shifted dramatically. Their previous hostility melted into gratitude.

With the crisis resolved, one mystery lingered: Jax Dunn's obsession with the metal sheet. Did he, too, sense the box's extraordinary potential? How he came to know of its existence remained an enigma.

And the box itself? An artifact of technological prowess beyond our time, an unparalleled electronic marvel. I consigned it to the depths of the Pacific, casting it overboard during my voyage home, wishing it to vanish like the high priest's forgotten tomb—its secrets submerged, never to be unearthed again.

www.ingramcontent.com/pod-product-compliance
Lightning Source LLC
Chambersburg PA
CBHW061121310726
48974CB00002B/627